BEFORE HE FEELS

(A MACKENZIE WHITE MYSTERY—BOOK 6)

BLAKE PIERCE

D1189725

ISBN: 978-1-64029-077-8

BOOKS BY BLAKE PIERCE

RILEY PAIGE MYSTERY SERIES
ONCE GONE (Book #1)
ONCE TAKEN (Book #2)
ONCE CRAVED (Book #3)
ONCE LURED (Book #4)
ONCE HUNTED (Book #5)
ONCE PINED (Book #6)
ONCE FORSAKEN (Book #7)
ONCE COLD (Book #8)
ONCE STALKED (Book #9)
ONCE LOST (Book #10)

MACKENZIE WHITE MYSTERY SERIES
BEFORE HE KILLS (Book #1)
BEFORE HE SEES (Book #2)
BEFORE HE COVETS (Book #3)
BEFORE HE TAKES (Book #4)
BEFORE HE NEEDS (Book #5)
BEFORE HE FEELS (Book #6)

AVERY BLACK MYSTERY SERIES
CAUSE TO KILL (Book #1)
CAUSE TO RUN (Book #2)
CAUSE TO HIDE (Book #3)
CAUSE TO FEAR (Book #4)
CAUSE TO SAVE (Book #5)

KERI LOCKE MYSTERY SERIES
A TRACE OF DEATH (Book #1)
A TRACE OF MUDER (Book #2)
A TRACE OF VICE (Book #3)
A TRACE OF CRIME (Book #4)

PROLOGUE

He'd read the book at least a dozen times, but that was okay. It was a good book and he had even gone so far as to give each character his or her own voice. It also helped that it was one of his favorites—*Something Wicked This Way Comes* by Ray Bradbury. To most, it might seem like an odd book to read to the residents of a home for the blind, but everyone he'd ever read it to seemed to like it.

He was nearing the end, and his latest resident was eating it up. Ellis, a fifty-seven-year-old woman, had told him she'd been born blind and lived the past eleven years in the home, after her son had decided he didn't want the baggage of a blind mother anymore, and placed her in the Wakeman Home for the Blind.

Ellis seemed to like him right away. She'd later told him that she told very few of the other residents about him because she enjoyed having him to herself. And that was fine with him. As a matter of fact, that was pretty much perfect as far as he was concerned.

Even better, about three weeks ago she had insisted that they leave the grounds of the home; she wanted to enjoy his storytelling in the fresh air, with the breeze on her face. And while there wasn't much of a breeze today—it was, actually, gruelingly hot—that was fine by him. They were sitting in a small rose garden about half a mile away from the home. It was, she'd said, a place she visited a lot. She liked the smell of the roses and the buzzing of the bees.

And now, his voice, telling her Ray Bradbury's story.

He was glad that she liked him so much. He liked her, too. Ellis didn't interrupt his reading with hundreds of questions like some of the others did. She simply sat there, looking into space she had never properly seen, and hung on each and every word.

As he came to the end of a chapter, he checked his watch. He had already stayed ten minutes beyond his usual time. He didn't have any others he planned to visit today, but he did have plans for later in the evening.

Placing his bookmark between the pages, he set the book down. Without the story to distract him, he realized just how oppressive the southern heat was on his back.

"Is that it for today?" Ellis asked.

He smiled at the observation. It never failed to amaze him how well the other senses made up for lack of sight. She'd heard him shift on the small bench near the center of the garden, then the soft noise of the book being placed on his leg.

"Yeah, I'm afraid so," he said. "I've already worn out my welcome by ten minutes."

"How much is left?" she asked.

"About forty pages. So we'll knock it out next week. Sound good?"

"Sounds perfect," she said. She then frowned slightly and added: "Do you mind if I ask you…well, you know…it's so dumb, but…"

"No, that's fine, Ellis."

He leaned in close to her and let her touch his face. She ran her hands along the contours of it. He understood the need for it (and Ellis wasn't the only blind woman who had done this to him) but it still weirded him out. A brief smile came to her mouth as she made her way around his head and then removed her hands.

"Thanks," she said. "And thanks for reading. I was wondering if you had any ideas for the next book?"

"Depends what you're in the mood for."

"A classic, maybe?"

"This is Ray Bradbury," he said. "That's about as classic as I get. I do think I have *The Lord of the Flies* lying around somewhere."

"That's the one about the boys stranded on the island, right?"

"Boiled down, yes."

"Sounds good. But this one…this *Something Wicked This Way Comes* is brilliant. Great choice!"

"Yeah, it's one of my favorites."

He was rather glad that she could not see the devious smile on his face. *Something wicked this way comes, indeed,* he thought.

He picked up his book, well-worn and battered from years of use, first opened about thirty years ago. He waited for her to stand with him, like an impatient date. She had her walking stick with her but she rarely used it.

The walk back to the Wakeman Home for the Blind was a short one. He liked to watch the look of concentration on her face as she started walking. He wondered what it must be like to rely on all of your other senses to move around. It must be exhausting to maneuver around a world without being able to see it.

As he studied her face, he hoped, most of all, that Ellis had enjoyed what she'd heard of the book.

He held his book tightly, almost a little disappointed that Ellis would never find out how it ended.

2

Ellis found herself thinking of the young boys from *Something Wicked This Way Comes.* It was October in the book. She wished it was October here. But no…it was the end of July in southern Virginia, and she didn't think it could get any hotter. Even after planning her walk just before twilight, the temperature was still a cruel ninety degrees according to Siri on her iPhone.

Sadly, she had come to know Siri well. She was a great way to pass the time, speaking in her snooty little robotic voice, filling Ellis in on trivia, weather updates, and sports scores.

There were a few tech people at the home who always made sure all of her computer gadgets were updated. She had a MacBook stocked with iTunes and a pretty substantial music library. She also had the latest iPhone and even a top-of-the-line app that responded to an attached gadget that allowed her to interact in Braille.

Siri had just told her that it was eighty-seven degrees outside. That seemed impossible, seeing as how it was almost 7:30 in the evening. *Ah well,* she thought. *A little sweat never hurt anyone.*

She thought about just forgetting her walk. It was a walk she took at least five times a week. And she'd already taken it once today to meet with the man who read to her. She didn't need the exercise but…well, she had certain rituals and routines. It made her feel normal. It made her feel sane. Plus, there was something to the sound of the afternoon while the sun was setting. She could *feel* it setting and *hear* something like a soft electric hum in the air as the world fell quiet, pulling dusk in with night on its heels.

So she decided to go for a walk. Two people within the home said goodbye to her, familiar voices—one filled with boredom, the other with a dulled cheer. She relished the feel of fresh air on her face as she stepped out onto the main lawn.

"Where the hell are you going, Ellis?"

It was another familiar voice—the manager of Wakeman, a jolly man named Randall Jones.

"My usual walk," she answered.

"It's so hot, though! You be quick about it. I don't want you passing out!"

"Or missing my ridiculous curfew," she said.

"Yeah, or that," Randall said with a bit of scorn.

She carried on with her walk, feeling the looming presence of the home fall away behind her. She felt an open space ahead of her, the lawn waiting for her. Beyond that was the sidewalk and, half a mile later, the rose garden.

Ellis hated the idea that she was nearing sixty and had a curfew. She understood it, but it made her feel like a child. Still, other than her lack of sight, she had it pretty sweet at the Wakeman Home for the Blind. She even had that nice man who came in to read to her once a week—and sometimes twice. She knew that he read to a few others, too. But those were people at other homes. Here at Wakeman, she was the only one he read to. It made her feel special. It made her feel like he preferred her. He'd complained to her that most of the others enjoyed romance novels or best-seller drivel. But with Ellis, he could read things he enjoyed. Two weeks ago, they'd finished up *Cujo* by Stephen King. And now there was this Bradbury book and—

She paused in her walk, cocking her head slightly.

She thought she'd heard something close to her. But after pausing, she did not hear it again.

Probably just an animal passing through the woods on my right, she thought. It was southern Virginia after all…and there were lots of woods and lots of critters living in them.

She tapped her cane out ahead of her, finding a weird sort of comfort in its familiar *click click* noise as it struck the sidewalk. While she obviously had never seen the sidewalk or the road alongside of it, they had been described to her several times. She'd also put something of a mental picture together in her mind, connecting smells with the descriptions of flowers and trees that some of the home's aides and caretakers had given her.

Within five minutes, she could smell the roses several yards ahead. She could hear the bees buzzing around them. Sometimes she thought she could even smell the bees, covered in pollen and whatever honey they were producing elsewhere.

She knew the path to the rose garden so well that she could have made her way around it without the use of her cane. She'd lapped it at least one thousand times in the course of her eleven years at the home. She came out here to reflect on her life, how things had gotten so difficult that her husband had left her fifteen years ago and then her son eleven years ago. She didn't miss her bastard of an ex-husband at all, but she did miss the feel of a man's hands on her. If she was being honest with herself, it was one of the reasons she enjoyed feeling the face of the man who read to her. He had a strong chin, high cheekbones, and one of those southern drawls to his voice that was addictive to listen to. He could read her the phone book and she'd enjoy it.

4

She was thinking of him as she felt herself enter the familiar contours of the garden. The concrete was crisp and hard under her feet but everything else in front of her felt soft and inviting. She paused for a moment and discovered that, as was usually the case in the afternoons, she had the place to herself. No one else was there.

Again, she stopped. She heard something behind her.

Feel it, too, she thought.

"Who is that?" she asked.

She got no answer. She had come out this late because she knew the garden would be deserted. Very few came out after six in the afternoon because the town of Stateton, in which the Wakeman Home for the Blind was located, was a tiny speck of a place. When she had stepped outside fifteen minutes ago, she'd listened for the movement of anyone else who might be out on the front lawn and had heard no one. She'd also heard no one else on the sidewalk as she had come down to the garden. There was the possibility that someone could be out with the intention of sneaking up on her and scaring her, but that could be risky. There were repercussions to such behavior in this town, laws that were enforced by a tried and true southern police force that didn't take shit when it came to local teens and bullies trying to pick on the disabled.

But there it was again.

She heard the noise, and the feeling that someone was there was stronger now. She smelled someone. It was not a bad smell at all. In fact, it was familiar.

Fear ran through her then, and she opened her mouth to yell.

But before she could, suddenly, she felt an immense pressure around her throat. She felt something else, too, radiating off of the person like heat.

Hate.

She gagged, unable to yell, to speak, to breathe, and she felt herself sinking to her knees.

The pressure tightened around her throat and that feeling of hate seemed to penetrate her, as pain spread throughout her body, and for the first time, Ellis was relieved that she was blind. As she felt her life slipping from her, she was relieved she would not have to lay eyes upon the face of evil. Instead, she had only that all-too-familiar darkness behind her eyes to welcome her into whatever awaited her after this life.

CHAPTER ONE

Mackenzie White, always on the go, was perfectly happy being confined to her little cubicle space. She was even happier when, three weeks ago, McGrath had called her up and told her that there was a vacant office thanks to a round of government layoffs, and that it was hers if she wanted it. She'd waited a few days, and when no one else had taken it, she went ahead and moved in.

It was minimally decorated, with only her desk, a floor lamp, a small bookshelf, and two chairs across from her desk. A large dry-erase calendar hung on the wall. She was staring at the calendar as she took a break between answering emails and making calls in her attempt to find details about one particular case.

It was an older case...a case linked to the single business card that she had on the dry-erase calendar, hanging there by a magnet:

Barker Antiques

It was the name of a business that apparently never existed.

Any lines of investigation that popped up were usually dashed right away. The closest they had come to getting anywhere was when Agent Harrison had discovered a place in New York that was a possible link. But that had turned out to be nothing more than a man who had sold old knock-off antiques in his garage in the late '80s.

Still, there was the sense that she was *this* close to finding some thread that would lead her to the answers she had been looking for—answers regarding the death of her father and the apparently linked murder that had occurred earlier in the year, just six months ago.

She tried holding on to that sense of something being out there, dangling unseen yet somehow also right in front of her face. She had to on days like today when she'd had three possible leads die in their tracks via phone calls and emails.

The business card had become a puzzle piece to her. She stared at it every day, trying to figure out some approach she had not yet tried.

She was so enamored with it that when someone knocked on her office door, she jumped a bit. She looked to the door and saw Ellington standing there. He poked his head in and looked around.

"Yeah, an office setting still doesn't suit you."

"I know," Mackenzie said. "I feel like such a fraud. Come on in."

"Oh, I don't have a lot of time," he said. "I was just wondering if you might want to get lunch."

"I can do that," she said. "Meet me downstairs in about half an hour and—"

Her desk phone rang, interrupting her. She read the display and saw that it was coming from McGrath's extension. "One second," she said. "This is McGrath."

Ellington nodded and made a playfully stern face.

"This is Agent White," she said.

"White, it's McGrath. I need to see you in my office as soon as possible about a new assignment. Round up Ellington and bring him with you."

She opened her mouth to say *Yes sir,* but McGrath killed the call before she could so much as draw up a breath.

"Looks like lunch has to wait," she said. "McGrath needs to see us."

They shared an awkward glance as the same thought passed between them. They'd often wondered how long they'd be able to keep their romantic relationship a secret from their co-workers, particularly McGrath.

"You think he knows?" Ellington asked.

Mackenzie shrugged. "I don't know. But he did say he needs to see us about an assignment. So if he *does* know, that's apparently not the purpose behind the call."

"Let's go find out then," Ellington said.

Mackenzie logged out of her computer and joined Ellington as they headed through the building and toward McGrath's office. She tried to tell herself that she really didn't care if McGrath knew about them. It wasn't grounds for suspension or anything like that, but he would likely never allow them to work again if he *did* find out.

So while she tried her best to not care, there was also some worry there. She did her best to swallow it down as they neared McGrath's office while trying to purposefully walk as far away from Ellington as possible.

***

McGrath eyed them suspiciously as they took the two seats across from his desk. It was a seat Mackenzie was growing used to, sitting there and getting either lectured or praised by McGrath. She

7

wondered which it would be today before he handed them their assignment.

"So, let's deal with some housekeeping first," McGrath said. "It's become clear to me that there's something going on between you two. I don't know if it's love or just a fling or what…and I honestly don't care. But this is your one and only warning. If it gets in the way of your work, you'll never be partnered up again. And that would be a damned shame because you work really well together. Am I understood?"

Mackenzie didn't see the point in denying it. "Yes sir."

Ellington echoed her response and she smirked when she saw that he looked embarrassed. She figured he wasn't the sort who was used to getting reprimanded by those above him.

"Now that we have *that* out of the way, let's get to the case," McGrath said. "We got a call from the sheriff of a small southern town called Stateton. There's a home for the blind located there—and that's about all there is, from what I gather. Last night, a blind woman was killed extremely close to the premises. And while that's certainly tragic enough, it's the second murder of a blind person in the state of Virginia within ten days. In both cases, there appears to be trauma to the neck, indicating strangulation, as well as irritation around the eyes."

"Was the first victim a member of a home as well?" Mackenzie asked.

"Yes, though a much smaller one from what I gather. It was originally speculated that the killer was a family member, but it took less than a week for everyone to be cleared. With a second body and what appears to be a very specific set of targets, it's likely not just coincidental. So you can understand the urgency of this situation, I hope. Honestly, I get a creeping sort of small town feel to this one. Not many people down there, so it should be easier to find a suspect quickly. I'm assigning this to the two of you because I fully expect you to have it wrapped within forty-eight hours. Less would be even better."

"Is Agent Harrison not being involved on this one?" Mackenzie asked. Having not spoken to him since the passing of his mother, she felt almost guilty. While he had never truly felt like a partner, she still respected him.

"Agent Harrison has been tasked elsewhere," McGrath said. "For this case, he will be a resource to you…research, expedited information, and things of that nature. Are you uncomfortable working with Agent Ellington?"

"Not at all, sir," she said, regretting that she had said anything at all.

"Good. I'll have human resources book you a room in Stateton. I'm not an idiot...so I've requested just one room. If nothing else comes out of this little fling between the two of you, at least it will save the bureau on lodging costs."

Mackenzie wasn't sure if this was McGrath's attempt at humor. It was hard to tell because the man seemed to never smile.

As they got up to head out on their assignment, it occurred to Mackenzie how vague McGrath's response about Harrison had been. *He's been tasked somewhere else,* Mackenzie thought. *What's that supposed to mean?*

That wasn't for her to be concerned with, though. Instead, she had been assigned a case that McGrath was expecting a quick turnaround on. Already, she could feel the challenge brewing inside of her, pushing her to get started right away.

CHAPTER TWO

Mackenzie felt a chill pass through her as Ellington guided them down State Route 47, deeper into the heart of rural Virginia. A few cornfields popped up here and there, breaking the monotony of sprawling fields and forests. The number of cornfields was no match for what she was used to in Nebraska, but the sight of them still made her a bit uneasy.

Luckily, the closer they got to the town of Stateton, the fewer cornfields she saw. They were replaced by freshly leveled acres of land that had been torn up by local lumber companies. In doing research on the area on the four-and-a-half-hour drive down, she'd seen where there was a fairly large lumber distributor in a neighboring town. As for the town of Stateton, though, it was the Wakeman Home for the Blind, a few antique stores, and very little else.

"Anything those case files tell you that I'm not privy to yet? It's hard to read the constant flow of emails from over here in the driver's seat."

"Nothing, really," she said. "It looks like we'll need to go through the same procedures as always. Visiting the families, the home for the blind, things like that."

"Visiting the families...should be easy in an inbred little town like this, huh?"

She was shocked at first but then let it pass. She had learned after a few weeks together as what she supposed could be considered "a couple" that Ellington had a relatively active sense of humor; it could be dry at times, though.

"You ever spend much time in a place like this?" Mackenzie asked.

"Summer camp," Ellington said. "It's a chunk of my teenage years I'd really like to forget. You? Was it ever this bad out in Nebraska?"

"Not quite like this, but it was desolate sometimes. There are times when I think I prefer the quiet out here, in places like this, more than I enjoy the packed traffic and people in places like DC."

"Yeah, I think I could see that."

It was fun for Mackenzie to be able to get to know Ellington better without the trappings of a traditional dating relationship. Rather than learning about one another over fancy dinners or long walks in a park, they had gotten to know one another over car rides and time spent in FBI offices or conferences rooms. And she'd enjoyed every minute of it. Sometimes she wondered if she'd ever get tired of getting to know him.

So far, she wasn't sure it would be possible.

Up ahead, a small sign along the side of the road welcomed them to Stateton, Virginia. A simple two-lane road led them through more trees. A few houses and their lawns broke the monotony of the forest for about a mile or so before any real signs of a town took over. They passed by a greasy spoon–type diner, a barbershop, two antique stores, a farm supply store, two mini-marts, a post office, and then, about two miles beyond all of that, a perfectly square brick building just off the main road. A very military-style sign out front read Staunton County Police Department and Correctional Facility

"Ever seen that before?" Ellington asked. "A police department and the county jail in one building?"

"A few times in Nebraska," she said. "I think it's pretty common in places like these. The closest actual prison to Stateton is in Petersburg, and that's about eighty miles away, I think."

"Jesus, this place *is* small. We should have this wrapped up pretty quickly."

Mackenzie nodded as Ellington turned into the driveway and into the parking lot of the large brick building that looked as if it sat literally in the middle of nowhere.

What she was thinking but did not say was: *I hope you didn't just jinx us.*

***

Mackenzie smelled dark coffee and something like Febreeze when they stepped into the small lobby at the front of the building. It looked quite nice inside, but it was an old building. Its age could be seen in the ceiling cracks and the obvious need for new carpet in the lobby. An enormous desk sat along the far wall and while it also looked as old as the rest of the building, it looked well-kept.

An older woman sat behind the desk, sorting through a large binder. When she heard Mackenzie and Ellington enter, she looked up with a huge smile. It was a beautiful smile but it also showed her age. Mackenzie guessed her to be reaching seventy.

"You the agents with the FBI?" the aging lady asked.

"Yes ma'am," Mackenzie said. "I'm Agent White and this is my partner, Agent Ellington. Is the sheriff around?"

"He is," she said. "In fact, he's asked me to direct you straight to his office. He's quite busy fielding calls about this latest horrible

11

death. Just head down to the corridor to your left. His office is the last door on the right."

They followed her directions and as they headed down the long corridor that led to the back of the building, Mackenzie was taken aback by the silence of the place. In the midst of a murder case, she'd expected the place to be abuzz with activity, even if it *was* the middle of nowhere.

As they headed for the back of the corridor, Mackenzie noticed a few signs that had been posted on the walls. One said: **Prison Access Requires Keycard.** Another read: **All Prison Visits Must Be Cleared by County Officials! Approval Must Be Presented At Time of Visit!**

Her mind started to race with thoughts of the maintenance and regulations that must have to be in place for a prison and a police department to share the same space. It was quite fascinating to her. But before her mind could get going any further, they reached the office at the back of the corridor.

Gold letters had been painted on the upper glass portion of the door, reading *Sheriff Clarke.* The door was partially open, so Mackenzie slowly opened it to the sound of a man's burly voice. When she peeked inside, she saw a heavyset man behind a desk, speaking loudly into his desk phone. Another man was sitting in a chair in the corner, furiously texting something on his cell phone.

The man behind the desk—Sheriff Clarke, Mackenzie presumed—interrupted himself on the phone as she opened the door.

"One minute, Randall," he said. He then covered the mouthpiece and looked back and forth between Mackenzie and Ellington.

"You with the bureau?" he asked.

"We are," Ellington said.

"Thank God," he sighed. "Give me a second." He then uncapped the mouthpiece and continued with his other conversation. "Look, Randall, the cavalry just arrived. Will you be available in fifteen minutes? Yeah? Okay, good. See you then."

The heavyset man hung up the phone and came around the desk. He offered a meaty hand to them, approaching Ellington first. "Good to meet you," he said. "I'm Sheriff Robert Clarke. This," he said, nodding toward the man sitting in the corner, "is Officer Keith Lambert. My deputy is out patrolling the streets right now, doing his best to find *some* sort of lead on this rapidly growing clusterfuck."

He nearly forgot about Mackenzie when he was done shaking Ellington's hand, offering another handshake to her almost as an afterthought. When she shook it, she did the intros, hoping it would clue him in to the fact that she was just as capable of leading this investigation as the men in the room. Instantly, old ghosts from Nebraska started rattling the chains in her head.

"Sheriff Clarke, I'm Agent White and this is Agent Ellington. Will you be our liaison here in Stateton?"

"Sweetie, I'll be just about your everything while you're here," he said. "The police force for the entire county numbers a whopping twelve people. Thirteen if you count Frances out there at the front desk and dispatch. With this murder spree going on, we're spread just a little thin."

"Well, let's see what we can do to lighten your load," Mackenzie said.

"I wish it was that easy," he said. "Even if we solve this fucking thing today, I'm going to have half the board of supervisors for the county up my ass."

"Why is that?" Ellington asked.

"Well, the local papers just got wind of who the victim was. Ellis Ridgeway. The mother of an up-and-coming scum-sucking douchebag politician. Some say he might make the senate within another five years."

"And who is that?" Mackenzie asked.

"Langston Ridgeway. Twenty-eight years old and thinks he's John Fucking Kennedy."

"Is that so?" Mackenzie said, a little shocked that had not been included in the reports.

"Yeah. How the local paper got that information is beyond me. The morons can't spell right half the time, but this they get."

"I saw signs for the Wakeman Home for the Blind on our way in," Mackenzie said. "It's only six miles from here, is that correct?"

"On the money," Clarke said. "I was just talking to Randall Jones, the manager over there. That's who I was on the phone with when you came in. He's over there right now to answer any questions you have. And the sooner the better. He's got the press and some county bigwigs calling him and bugging the shit out of him."

"Well, let's head over there," Mackenzie said. "Will you be coming with us?"

"No way, sweetie. I'm swamped as it is here. But please do come back by when you're done with Randall. I'll help you however I can but really…I'd love for you two to take this ball and run with it."

"No problem," Mackenzie said. She wasn't quite sure how to handle Clarke. He was up front and bluntly honest, which was good. He also seemed to really love dropping curse words. She also thought that when he called her *sweetie,* he wasn't being insulting. It was that weird sort of southern charm.

Also, the man was stressed beyond his means.

"We'll come right back here when we're done at the home," Mackenzie said. "Please call us if you hear anything new between now and then."

"Of course," Clarke said.

In the corner, still texting on his phone, Officer Lambert grunted in agreement.

Having spent less than three minutes in Sheriff Clarke's office, Mackenzie and Ellington walked back down the corridor and exited through the lobby. The older woman, whom Mackenzie assumed was the Frances that Clarke had mentioned, waved at them briskly as they made their exit.

"Well, that was…interesting," Ellington said.

"The man is in over his head," she said. "Give him a break."

"You just like him because he calls you *sweetie,"* Ellington said.

"And?" she said with a smile.

"Hey, I can start calling you sweetie."

"Please don't," she said as they got into the car.

Ellington drove them half a mile down Highway 47 and then took a left onto a back road. Right away, they saw a sign for the Wakeman Home for the Blind. As they got closer to the property, Mackenzie started to wonder why someone would have chosen such a random and isolated location for a home for the blind. Surely there was some sort of psychological meaning behind it. Perhaps being located in the middle of nowhere helped them to relax, removed from the constant droning noises of a larger city.

All she knew for sure was that as the trees grew thicker around them, she started to feel more choked off from the rest of the world. And for the first time in a very long time, she almost yearned for the familiar sights of those cornfields of her youth.

CHAPTER THREE

The Wakeman Home for the Blind did not look at all like Mackenzie was expecting. In contrast to the Staunton County Police Department and Correctional Facility, the Wakeman Home for the Blind looked like a marvel of modern design and construction—and that was a view Mackenzie arrived at before they even stepped foot inside.

The front of the place was made of large glass windows that seemed to make up the majority of the walls. Halfway down the sidewalk toward the entrance, Mackenzie could already see inside. She saw a large lobby that looked like something straight out of some sort of spa. It was friendly looking and inviting.

It was a feeling that only intensified once they stepped inside. Everything was very clean and looked new. In the research she had done on the way to Stateton, she'd discovered that the Wakeman Home for the Blind had only just been built in 2007. When it had been built, there had been a slight hurrah within Staunton County, as it brought in new jobs and commerce. Now, however, while it was still one of the more prominent buildings in the county, the excitement had died down and the home seemed to have gotten swallowed up by its rural surroundings.

A young woman sat behind a curved counter along the back wall. She greeted them with a smile, though it was clear that she was troubled. Mackenzie and Ellington approached her, introduced themselves, and were promptly asked to take a seat in the waiting area while Randall Jones came out to meet them.

As it turned out, Randall Jones was very anxious to meet with them. Mackenzie had been sitting for no more than ten seconds before a set of double doors leading to the back of the building opened up on the other side of the waiting room. A tall man wearing a button-down shirt and khakis stepped through. He tried on a smile as he introduced himself, but, just like the receptionist, he could not hide the fact that he was tired and very troubled.

"I'm glad you're here so soon," Jones said. "The sooner we can get this wrapped up, the better. The small-town grapevine is on fire with this one."

"We'd like to get it knocked out as soon as possible as well," Mackenzie said. "Do you know exactly where the body was found?"

"Yes. It's a rose garden about half a mile from here. It was originally going to be the site for Wakeman but some weird county zoning regulations messed it all up."

"Could you take us there?" Mackenzie asked.

"Of course. Anything you need. Come with me."

Jones led them through the double doors he had come through. On the other side, there was a very small alcove that led directly into the home. The first few doors they passed were offices and storage spaces. These were separated from the residents' rooms by an open office area where one man and one woman sat behind a counter space much like a hospital wing.

As they passed by the rooms, Mackenzie peeked inside one that was open. The rooms were quite spacious and decked out with nice furniture. She also saw laptops and smartpads in a few of the rooms.

Despite being located in the middle of nowhere, there apparently isn't a shortage of funds to keep the placing going, she thought.

"How many residents live here?" Mackenzie asked.

"Twenty-six," he said. "And they come from all over. We have one older man who came all the way from California because of the exceptional service and quality of life we can offer."

"Forgive me if it's an ignorant question," Mackenzie said, "but what sort of things do they do?"

"Well, we have classes that cover a wide variety of interests. Most have to be specialized to cater to their needs, of course. We have cooking classes, exercise programs, a board game club, trivia clubs, gardening classes, crafts, things like that. Also, a few times out of the year, we organize outings to allow them to hike or swim. We even have two brave souls who have taken to canoeing whenever we go out."

Hearing all of this made Mackenzie feel both insensitive, yet happy as well. She had no idea that people who were completely blind could become adept at things like canoeing or swimming.

Near the end of the hallway, Jones brought them to an elevator. When they stepped inside and headed down, Jones leaned against the wall, clearly exhausted.

"Mr. Jones," Mackenzie said, "do you have any idea how the local papers would have already learned about the murder?"

"No idea," he said. "That's one of the reasons I'm so tired. I've been extensively questioning my staff. But everyone checks out. There's certainly a leak but I have no idea where it's coming from."

Mackenzie nodded. *Not really much of a concern there,* she thought. *A leak in a little town like this is almost a certainty. It shouldn't get in the way of the investigation, though.*

The elevator came to a stop and let them out at a small finished basement of sorts. A few chairs were spread out here and there but Jones led them to a door straight ahead of them. They stepped outside and Mackenzie found herself behind the building, facing an employee parking lot.

Randall led them to his car and when they got in, he wasted no time blasting the air conditioning. The inside of the car was like a furnace, but the air started its work right away.

"How did Mrs. Ridgeway get to the garden?" Ellington asked.

"Well, being that we're in the middle of nowhere, we do allow our residents a certain amount of freedom. We have a curfew of nine o'clock during the summer—which drops to six o' clock in the fall and winter when it gets dark earlier. The rose garden we're headed to is a spot some of the residents go just to get out. As you'll see, it's a quick walk without any hazards."

Randall backed them out of the lot and turned onto the road. He was headed in the opposite direction of the police department, revealing a new stretch of the road to Mackenzie and Ellington.

The road was a straight stretch that veered farther back into the woods. But within thirty seconds, Mackenzie could see the small cast-iron gates that bordered the rose garden. Randall pulled into a thin strip of a parking lot where there were only three other cars parked, one of which was an unattended police car.

"Sheriff Clarke and his men have been out here most of last night and early this morning," Randall said. "When he heard you guys were coming, he had it abandoned. He really doesn't want to get in the way, you know?"

"We certainly appreciate that," Mackenzie said, stepping out of the car and back into the stifling heat.

"We know for a fact that this was the last place Ellis Ridgeway visited," Randall said. "She passed two other residents on her way out, as well as me. Further proof of this can be seen on the security cameras at the home. She's very obviously heading in this direction—and everyone in the home knows she liked to take late evening walks here. She did it at least four or five times on most weeks."

"And no one else was here with her?" Mackenzie asked.

"Not anyone from the home. Honestly, not many people come out here in the dead center of summer. I'm sure you've noticed that we're in the middle of a pretty rough hot spell."

As they came to the east side of the garden, Mackenzie was almost overwhelmed with the smells. She caught whiffs of roses, hydrangeas, and what she thought might be lavender. She supposed it must be a nice getaway for the blind—a way to truly enjoy their other senses.

When they reached a bend in the trail that curved farther back to the east, Jones turned and pointed back behind them. "If you look through that break in the trees on the other side of the road, you can see the backside of Wakeman," he said sadly. "She was *this* close to us when she died."

He then stepped off of the walkway and squeezed past two large flowerpots containing red roses. Mackenzie and Ellington followed him. They reached a back gate that had been mostly hidden by all of the flowers, trees, and vegetation. There was a space of about four feet that was empty, save for some stray grass.

As they walked through, she could instantly see how it might seem like a perfect place for a patient killer to strike. Randall Jones had said it himself—no one came out here much when it got so hot. The killer certainly knew about this and used it to his advantage.

"This is where I found her," Jones said, pointing to the empty space between the larger pots and the black cast-iron gates. "She was lying face down and bent into a sort of U shape."

"*You* found her?" Ellington asked.

"Yes. At about nine forty-five last night. When she didn't make it back for curfew, I started to worry. After half an hour, I figured I should come check to see if she'd fallen or panicked or something."

"Were all of her clothes in place?" Mackenzie asked.

"As far as I could tell," Randall said, clearly surprised by the question. "In the moment, I wasn't really thinking in such a way."

"And there's absolutely no one else on that video footage at the home?" Ellington asked. "No one following her?"

"No one. You're welcome to look at the footage for yourself when we get back."

As they headed back through the garden, Ellington brought up a question that had been brewing on Mackenzie's mind. "It seems very quiet today in the home. What gives?"

"I guess you'd call it mourning. We have a very tight-knit community at Wakeman and Ellis was so loved. Very few of our residents have come out of their rooms all day. We also made an announcement over the PA that we'd have agents from DC coming to look into Ellis's murder. Ever since then, hardly anyone has come out of their room. I guess they're freaked out…scared."

That, plus no one following her out of the home rules out the murderer being a resident, Mackenzie thought. The meager file on the first victim stated that the murder occurred between eleven o'clock and midnight...and a pretty good distance away from Stateton.

"Would it be at all possible for us to speak to some of your residents?" Mackenzie asked.

"It's absolutely fine with me," Jones said. "Of course, if they're uncomfortable with it I'll have to ask you to stop."

"Of course. I think I could—"

She was interrupted by the ringing of her phone. She checked it and saw an unfamiliar number in the display.

"One second," she said, taking the call. She turned away from Jones and answered: "This is Agent White."

"Agent White, it's Sheriff Clarke. Look, I know you just left here but I'd really appreciate it if you could hustle back down as soon as you can."

"Sure. Is everything okay?"

"It's been better," he said. "I've just got this jerk-off waste of space Langston Ridgeway down here. He's demanding to speak with you about his mother's case and he's starting to cause a bit of a scene."

Even in the sticks, you can't escape politics, Mackenzie thought.

Irritated, she did her best to respond in a professional manner. "Give us about ten minutes," she said and killed the call.

"Mr. Jones, we're going to have to head back to the sheriff for now," she said. "Could you have that security footage cued up for us when we come back?"

"Of course," Randall said, leading them back to his car.

"And in the meantime," Mackenzie added, "I want a list of anyone you have even the slightest suspicions about. I'm talking employees and other residents. People that would know the reach of the security camera in the garden."

Jones nodded somberly. The look on his face told Mackenzie that this was something he had considered himself but had not dared put much belief into. With that same expression on his face, he started the car and took them back to Wakeman. Along the way, Mackenzie again noticed the silence of the little town—not tranquil, but more like the calm before a storm.

CHAPTER FOUR

The first thought that popped into Mackenzie's head when she saw Langston Ridgeway was that he looked like a praying mantis. He was tall and skinny, and he moved his arms like awkward little pinchers when he talked. It didn't help that his eyes were huge with fury as he yelled at everyone who tried speaking to him.

Sheriff Clarke had ushered them into the small conference room at the end of the hallway—a room that wasn't much bigger than his office. Here, with the doors closed, Langston Ridgeway stood as tall as he could while Mackenzie and Ellington endured his wrath.

"My mother is dead and gone," he moaned, "and I'm inclined to blame the incompetence of the staff at the damned home. And since this sorry excuse for a sheriff refuses to let me speak to Randall Jones in person, I'd like to know what you two FBI goons intend to do about it."

Mackenzie waited a beat before responding. She was trying to gauge his level of grief. With the way he was behaving it was hard to tell if his anger was an expression of his loss or if he was genuinely just an atrocious man who liked to shout orders at others. So far, she couldn't tell.

"Quite frankly," Mackenzie said, "I agree with the sheriff. You're angry and hurt right now, and it seems like you're looking to pass blame. I am very sorry for your loss. But the worst thing you could do right now is to confront the management at the home."

"Blame?" Ridgeway asked, clearly not used to people not simply folding and agreeing with him right away. "If that place is responsible for what happened to my mother, then I—"

"We've already visited the home and spoken with Mr. Jones," Mackenzie said, cutting him off. "I can assure you that what happened to your mother was the influence of outside sources. And if it *is* internal, then Mr. Jones certainly knows nothing about it. I can tell you all of that with absolutely confidence."

Mackenzie wasn't sure if the look of shock that came over Ridgeway's face was the result of her disagreeing with him or because she had interrupted him.

"And you gathered all of that from one conversation?" he asked, clearly skeptical.

"I did," she said. "Of course, this investigation is still quite young so I can't be certain of anything. What I *can* tell you is that it's very hard to conduct an investigation when I get calls that end with me having to leave a crime scene just to listen to people yell and complain."

She could nearly feel the fury coming off of him now. "I just lost my mother," he said, each word like a whisper. "I want answers. I want justice."

"Good," Ellington said. "We want the same thing."

"But for us to get it," Mackenzie said, "you need to let us work. I understand you hold sway around here, but quite frankly, I don't care. We have a job to do and we can't let your anger, grief, or arrogance get in the way."

During the entire exchange, Sheriff Clarke sat at the small conference table. He was doing his very best to contain a smile.

Ridgeway was quiet for a moment. He looked back and forth between the agents and Sheriff Clarke. He nodded and when a tear slid down the side of his face, Mackenzie thought that it might be real. But she could also still see the anger in his eyes, right there at the surface.

"I'm sure you're used to throwing instructions around at small-town cops and suspects and whatnot," Langston Ridgeway said. "But let me tell you this…if you drop the ball on this case, or, for that matter, disrespect me again, I'll make a call to DC. I'll talk to your supervisor and bury you."

The sad thing is, he thinks he's fully capable of such a thing, Mackenzie thought. *And maybe he is. But I'd sure as hell love to be a fly on the wall when someone like Langston Ridgeway starts barking at McGrath.*

Rather than escalate the situation, Mackenzie decided to stay silent. She glanced beside her and saw that Ellington was clenching and unclenching his fist…a little trick he resorted to whenever he was on the verge of getting irrationally angry.

In the end, Mackenzie said, "If you let us do our job unhindered, it won't come to that."

It was clear that Ridgeway was searching for something else to say. All he could come up with was a muffled *hmmph*. He followed this by turning quickly away and leaving the room. It reminded Mackenzie very much of a child in the midst of a tantrum.

After a few seconds, Sheriff Clarke leaned forward with a sigh. "And now you see what I've been having to deal with. That boy thinks the sun rises and sets around his spoiled ass. And he can go on and on about losing his mother all he wants. All he's worried about is the media in bigger cities finding out that he dumped her in a home….even if it is a nice one. He's worried about his own image more than anything else."

21

"Yeah, I got that same feeling," Ellington said.

"Do you think we can expect any more interference from him?" Mackenzie asked.

"I don't know. He's unpredictable. He'll do whatever he thinks might improve his chances of getting public attention which will later turn to votes for whatever tainted sea he guns for."

"Well then, Sheriff," Mackenzie said, "if you have a few minutes, why don't we sit down and go over what we know?"

"That won't take long," he said. "Because there ain't much."

"That's better than nothing," Ellington said.

Clarke nodded and got to his feet. "Come on back to my office, then," he said.

As they made their way down the small hallway, both Mackenzie and Ellington jumped a bit when Clarke shouted, "Hey, Frances! Put on a pot of coffee, would you, darlin'?"

Mackenzie and Ellington exchanged a bewildered look. She was starting to get a very good feel for Sheriff Clarke and the way he ran things. And while they might be a bit rustic, she was finding that she liked him quite a bit—foul language and unintentional sexism aside.

With the evening inching closer to night, Mackenzie and Ellington huddled around Clarke's desk and went over the existing material on the case.

CHAPTER FIVE

Shortly before Frances brought in the coffee, Officer Lambert returned. Now that he was not texting on his phone, Mackenzie saw that he was a younger man, in his early thirties. She found it odd that an officer was serving as Clarke's right-hand man rather than a deputy but didn't think much of it.

Small town, she thought.

The four of them sat around Clarke's desk, going over the material. Clarke seemed to be more than happy to let Mackenzie run with it. She was happy to see that he appeared to be coming around quickly…accepting her as more than an equal.

"So let's start with the most recent," she said. "Ellis Ridgeway. Fifty-seven years old. As I'm beginning to learn, she has a very arrogant and self-important son. Other than the fact that she was obviously blind, what else can you tell me about her?"

"That's about it, really," Clarke said. "She was a sweet lady. From what I can gather, everyone at the home loved her. What scares me about this whole situation is that the killer has to be familiar with her, right? They had to have known she had left the home to target her in such a way."

"My brain wanted to go there, too," Mackenzie said. "But if these deaths are connected—and it certainly seems they are—that means that for someone local who knows her to have done it, there would have been a lot of traveling involved. The other death was what…two and a half hours away?"

"Almost three," Clarke said.

"Exactly," Mackenzie said. "You know, I even wondered for a while if it could have been another resident, but I got it on good authority from Randall Jones that no one followed her yesterday. There's apparently video evidence of this which we haven't seen yet, thanks to Langston Ridgeway's interference. And in terms of residents or employees leaving the home when Mrs. Ridgeway was absent, there is no evidence to support anyone else leaving during that time—not residents, not employees, no one."

"And then, going back to that first murder," Ellington said, "we'll need to head over to speak to family members soon. What can you tell us about the first victim, Sheriff?"

"Well, it was at another home for the blind," he said. "And all I know about it is in that same file you have, I'm sure. Like I said, it's almost three hours from here, nearly up in West Virginia. A

23

rundown sort of place from what I gather. Not really a home, but like a school, I think."

He slid a sheet of paper over to her and she saw the brief police report from the first scene. It was in a city called Treston, about twenty-five miles away from Bluefield, West Virginia. Thirty-eight-year-old Kenneth Able had been strangled to death. There were slight abrasions around his eyes. He'd been discovered stashed in the closet of the room he stayed in most of the time within the home.

The facts were very robotic, with no details. While there were notes about the investigation being ongoing, Mackenzie doubted it was anything serious.

I bet it is now, though, she thought.

This new death was too explicit to deny. The victims were far too similar, as were the signs of abuse on the bodies.

"I've got Randall Jones compiling a list of employees or others associated with the home that could be even the least bit possible," Mackenzie said. "I think our next best bet is to speak with this place in Treston to see if there are any links at all."

"The downside here is that Treston is so damned far away," Ellington pointed out. "Even if this turns out to be a cakewalk, there will be some travel involved. Seems we might not get it all buttoned up as quickly as the illustrious Mr. Ridgeway would like."

"When will a full forensics workup be done on Mrs. Ridgeway?" Mackenzie asked.

"I'm expecting to hear something within a few hours," Clarke said. "A preliminary investigation showed nothing obvious, though. No fingerprints, no visible hairs or other materials left behind." Mackenzie nodded and looked back to the case files. As she had just started to properly dig into it, her cell phone rang. She snatched it up and answered: "This is Agent White."

"It's Randall Jones. I have a list of names for you, like you asked. It's short and I'm pretty sure they'll all check out, though."

"Who are they?"

"There's a guy on the maintenance crew that isn't very reliable. He worked all day yesterday, clocking out just after five. I've asked around and no one ever saw him come back in. There's another man that works for a special outlet of social services. He comes in and plays board games sometimes. Sort of just hangs out and jokes around with them. He'll do some volunteer stuff like cleaning or moving furniture from time to time."

"Can you text me their names and any contact information you have?"

"Sure thing," Jones said, clearly not happy to even be considering either of the men as suspects.

Mackenzie ended the call and looked back to the three men in the room. "That was Jones with two possible candidates. A maintenance worker and someone that comes in to volunteer and hang out with the residents. Sheriff, he's going to text me the names any moment now. Could you look them over and—"

Her phone dinged as she received the text in question. She showed Sheriff Clarke the names and he shrugged, defeated.

"The first name, Mike Crews, is the maintenance guy," he said. "I know for a fact he wasn't killing anyone after hours last night because I had a beer with him down at Rock's Bar. That's *after* he went by Mildred Cann's house to fix her air conditioner for free. I can tell you right now that Mike Crews is not your man."

"And what about the second name?" Ellington asked.

"Robbie Huston," he said. "I've only ever seen him in passing. I'm pretty sure he's sent by some sort of social services outlet out of Lynchburg. But from what I understand, he's like a saint up at the home. Reads to the residents, is really friendly. Like I said, he's out of Lynchburg. That's about an hour and a half away from here— right on your way to Treston, as a matter of fact."

Mackenzie looked back to Jones's text and saved the number he had provided for Robbie Huston. It was a flimsy lead at best, but at least it was something.

She looked at her watch and saw that it was nearing six o'clock. "When are your deputy and other officers due to report back in?" she asked.

"Pretty soon. But no one has called in with anything yet. I'll keep you updated if you want to head out and get your bearings."

"Sounds good to me," Mackenzie said.

She gathered up the case files as she got to her feet. "Thanks for your help this afternoon," Mackenzie said.

"Of course. I just wish I could offer you more assistance. If you want, I could get the State PD back out here to assist. They were here this morning but scattered pretty quick. I think there might even be a few of them staying here in town for a day or so."

"If it comes to that, I'll let you know," Mackenzie said. "Good night, gentlemen."

With that, she and Ellington took their leave. The front lobby was empty now, Frances having apparently clocked out for the day.

In the parking lot, Ellington hesitated for a moment as he took the keys out. "Hotel or a trip to Lynchburg?" he asked.

She thought about it and although the lure of continuing the investigation even into the later hours was a strong one, she felt that trying to get in touch with Robbie Huston on the phone would yield the same results as a trip to Lynchburg. More than that, she was already starting to believe that Sheriff Clarke knew what he was doing—and if he had no real reservations about Huston, then she would rely on that for now. It was one of the better things about working a case in a small town—when everyone knew everyone else on an almost intimate basis, the opinions and instincts of local police could often be heavily relied upon.

Still worth calling him once we settle down, she thought.

"Hotel," she said. "If I can't get what I want out of a call to him tonight, we'll stop by Lynchburg tomorrow."

"On the way to Treston? Seems like a lot of driving."

She nodded. It *was* going to be a lot of back and forth. They may be more successful if they split up tomorrow. But they could discuss strategy after they were checked into a room with the case files before them and an air conditioner blasting away beside them.

Never one for the lure of luxury, the idea of an air conditioner in this oppressive heat was too good to resist. They got into the blazing hot car, Ellington rolled the windows down, and they headed west, into what served as the heart of Stateton.

***

Stateton's only motel was a surprisingly well-kept little square of a building called the Staunton County Inn. It held only twelve rooms, nine of which were vacant when Mackenzie walked into the lobby and requested a room for the night. Now that McGrath knew about their relationship, she and Ellington no longer worried about renting two rooms just to hold up appearances. They booked a single room with one bed and, after a stressful day of driving in the heat, made good use of it the moment the door closed behind them.

Afterward, as Mackenzie showered, she couldn't help but appreciate the warm feeling of being wanted. It was more than that, though; the fact that they had started peeling off clothes the moment they were alone and had access to a bed made her feel like she was about ten years younger. It was a good feeling, but one she tried very hard to keep in check. Yes, she was enjoying things with Ellington, and whatever was occurring between them was one of the most exciting and promising things to happen to her in recent years, but she also knew that if she wasn't careful she could let it interfere with her work.

She sensed that he knew this, too. He was risking the same things as she was: reputation, mockery, and heartbreak. Although lately, she wasn't sure if he was too worried about heartbreak. As she got to know him better, she was pretty sure Ellington was not the type of guy who slept around or treated women poorly, but she also knew that he had just come out of a failed marriage and was being very cautious about their relationship—if that's what they were choosing to call it.

She was getting the sense that Ellington would not be too shaken up if things ended between them. As for her...well, she wasn't sure how she might take it.

As she stepped out of the shower and dried off, Ellington was there, in the bathroom. It looked like he had planned to join her in the shower but had just missed his chance. He was giving her a look that held a bit of his usual slyness but also something concrete and stoic—something she had come to think of as his "work expression."

"Yes?" she asked playfully.

"Tomorrow...I don't want to do it, but maybe we should split up. One of us head up to Treston while the other stays here and works with the local PD and the coroner."

She smiled, realizing just how in sync they could become from time to time. "I was thinking the same thing."

"You have a preference?" he asked.

"Not really. I'll take Lynchburg and Treston. I don't mind driving."

She thought he was going to argue, wanting to take the time on the road instead. She knew he didn't particularly like driving, but he also didn't like the idea of her being out on the road all by herself.

"Sounds good," he said. "If we can wrap the day up with new information from the home in Treston with whatever information we get from the coroner down here, we could maybe get this thing tied up quickly like everyone is expecting."

"Sounds great," she said. She planted a kiss on his mouth as she passed by.

A thought passed through her mind as she headed back out into the room, one that made her feel almost lovesick but could not be denied.

What if he doesn't feel the same way about me as I feel about him?

He'd felt slightly distant over the last week or so, and while he had done his best to hide it from her, she'd seen it here and there.

Maybe he realizes just how much this could affect our work.

It was a good reason—a reason she often thought about herself. But she couldn't worry about that right now. With a coroner's report being delivered any moment now, this case had the potential to get rolling pretty quickly. And she knew that if her mind were on matters of Ellington and what they meant to one another, it might roll on by completely.

CHAPTER SIX

When they split up the following morning, Mackenzie was surprised to notice that Ellington seemed particularly somber about it. He hugged her a bit longer than usual in the motel room and looked rather depressed when she dropped him off at the Stateton PD. With a wave through the windshield as he walked inside, Mackenzie headed back for the main road with a two-hour-and-forty-minute drive ahead of her.

Being in the woods, the signal on her phone was spotty. She was not able to place a call to Jones's second potential suspect, Robbie Huston, until she was about ten miles outside of Stateton city limits. When she finally got the call to go through, he answered on the second ring.

"Hello?"

"Is this Robbie Huston?" she asked.

"It is. Who's asking?"

"This is Agent Mackenzie White with the FBI. I was wondering if you'd have time to chat this morning."

"Um…can I ask what about?"

His confusion and surprise were genuine. She could tell even over the phone.

"About a resident of the Wakeman Home for the Blind that I believe you know. I can't reveal more than that over the phone. If you could give me just five or ten minutes of your time this morning, I'd appreciate it. I'll be coming through Lynchburg in about an hour."

"Sure," he said. "I work from home, so you're welcome to just come by my apartment if you want."

She ended the call after she got his address. She plugged it into her GPS and was relieved to see that getting to his apartment would only add another twenty minutes to her drive.

On the way to Lynchburg, she found herself far too distracted by the facts of this current case, bogged down with the hundreds of unanswered questions surrounding her father's old case and the new death that had brought it back to light. For some reason, the same people who had killed her father had killed someone else in a very similar fashion.

And once again, they had left a cryptic business card behind. But why?

She'd spent weeks trying to figure it out. Maybe the killer was just cocky. Or maybe the cards were supposed to lead investigators to something else...like a twisted sort of cat and mouse game. She knew that Kirk Peterson was still on the case—a humble and dedicated private detective back in Nebraska whom she didn't know well enough to trust completely. Still, the fact that *someone* was actively keeping the trail as fresh as possible was reassuring. It made her feel like the puzzle might be nearly shut to her but that someone had snuck a piece off of the table and was holding on to it, determined to put it in at the very last moment.

She'd never felt so defeated by anything else in her life. It was no longer a question of whether or not she could bring her father's killer to justice, but more about putting a decades-old mystery to rest. As her mind was wrapped around it all, her phone started ringing. She saw an the sheriff's number in the display, answering and hoping for some sort of clue to the current case.

"G'morning, Agent White," Sheriff Clarke said on the other end. "Look, you know the cell reception down here in Stateton is crap. I've got Agent Ellington here, wanting to speak to you really quick. His cell phone couldn't get the call out."

She listened to the phone being jostled on the other end as it was handed over to Ellington. "So," he said. "Lost without me yet?"

"Hardly," she said. "I'm meeting with Robbie Huston in a little over an hour."

"Ah, progress. Speaking of which, I'm looking at the coroner's report right now. Hot off the presses. I'll let you know if I find anything. Randall Jones is coming in pretty soon, too. I might see if he'll let me speak to a few of the other residents up at the home."

"Sounds good. I'll be driving past cow pastures and empty fields for the next three hours."

"Ah, the glamorous life," he said. "Call if you need anything."

And with that, he ended the call.

This was how they exchanged barbs back and forth all of the time. It made her feel a little foolish for her earlier worries about how he was feeling about whatever it was that was evolving between them.

With the phone call having brought thoughts of her father's old case to a close, she was able to better focus on the case at hand. The digital thermometer on her car's dash told her that it was eight-eight degrees outside already...and it wasn't even nine o'clock yet.

The trees along the side of the back roads were impossibly thick, hanging over the road like an awning. And while there was something mysteriously pretty about them in the weak light of an early southern morning, she couldn't wait for the wider expanses of major highways and four lanes that would lead her toward Lynchburg and Treston.

***

Robbie Huston lived in a trendy little apartment complex near the central heart of Lynchburg. It was surrounded by college-owned bookshops and coffee corners that likely only thrived due to the large private Christian college that loomed over most of the city. When she knocked on his door at 9:52, he answered almost right away.

He looked to be in his early twenties—wiry, uncombed hair, and the sort of soft complexion that made Mackenzie think any work he'd ever done was from behind a desk. He was cute in a frat boy sort of way and was on the verge of either excitement or nervousness to actually have an FBI agent knocking on his door.

He invited her inside and she saw that the inside of the apartment was just as nice and modern as the outside. The living area, kitchen, and study were all one large room, separated by small ornate dividers and flooded with natural sunlight that poured in through two huge picture windows on opposite walls.

"Um...can I get you some coffee or something?" he asked. "I've still got some left in my morning pot."

"Coffee would be great, actually," she said.

She followed him into the kitchen where he poured her a cup and handed it to her. "Cream? Sugar?"

"No thanks," she said. She took a sip, found it quite good, and got to the point. "Mr. Huston, you often volunteer at the Wakeman Home for the Blind, is that correct?"

"Yes."

"About how often?"

"It depends on my workload, really. Sometimes I can only make it down once or twice a month. There have been months when I was able to make it down once a week, though."
"How about lately?" Mackenzie asked.

"Well, I was there on Monday of this week. Last week, I went on Wednesday and the week before that I was there on Monday and Friday, I think. I can show you my schedule."

"Maybe later," she said. "Speaking with Randall Jones, I found out that you will go to play board games and maybe help move furniture and clean. Is that right?"

"Yes, that's right. Every now and then I'll read to them, too."

31

"Them? Which residents in particular have you read to or played board games with in the past two weeks?"

"A few. There's an older gentleman by the name of Percy that I play Apples to Apples with. At least one caretaker has to play, too…to whisper what the cards say to him. And last week, I talked quite a bit with Ellis Ridgeway about music. I also read to her for a while."

"Do you know when you spent this time with Ellis?"

"The last two trips down there. Monday, I let her listen to Brian Eno. We talked about classical music and I read her an article online about some of the ways classical music is used to stimulate the brain."

Mackenzie nodded, knowing it was time to throw her biggest card on the table. "Well, I hate to tell you this, but Ellis was found murdered Tuesday night. We're trying to find out who did it, and as I'm sure you understand, we had to look into anyone who had spent time with her recently. Especially volunteers that aren't always in the home."

"Oh my God," Robbie said, his face going paler and paler by the moment.

"Before Mrs. Ridgeway, there was another murder in a home in Treston, Virginia. Have you ever been there?"

Robbie nodded. "Yes, but only twice. Once was for a sort of community service thing we do through Liberty, my alma mater. I helped remodel their kitchen and did some landscaping. I went back a month or two later to help where I could. It was mostly just relationship-building stuff."

"How long ago was this?"

He thought about it, still shaken by the news of the two murders. "Four years, I'd say. Maybe closer to four and a half."

"Do you recall meeting a man named Kenneth Able when you were there? He was also killed recently."

Again, he seemed lost in thought. His eyes almost seemed frozen. "The name doesn't sound familiar. But that doesn't mean I never spoke to him while I was there."

Mackenzie nodded, growing more and more certain that Robbie Huston was *far* from a killer. She couldn't be sure, but she thought she saw his eyes gleaming with tears as she gulped down some of the coffee he had given her.

Can't be too careful, though, she thought.

"Mr. Huston, we know for certain that Mrs. Ridgeway was killed half a mile away from Wakeman's grounds sometime between seven-oh-five and nine forty on Tuesday night. Do you have any sort of alibis for that stretch of time?"

She saw that searching look for a third time but then he started to nod very slowly. "I was here, in the apartment. I was on a conference call with three other guys. We're starting this small little organization to help the homeless downtown and in other surrounding cities."

"Any proof?"

"I could show you where I logged in. I think one of the other guys keeps pretty good notes of the calls, too. There will be all kind of time-stamped message threads, note edits, and things like that." He was already heading for his laptop, sitting on a desk in front of one of the large windows. "Here, I can show you if you want."

She was now positive that Robbie Huston was innocent but she wanted to see it through. Given the way the news had affected him, she also wanted Robbie to feel like he had contributed something to the case. So she watched over his shoulder as he went to the conference platform site, logged in, and pulled up his history not just for the last few days, but the last several weeks as well. She saw that he had been telling the truth: he'd been taking part in a conference call and planning session from 6:45 to 10:04 on Tuesday night.

The whole process took him less than five minutes to get through, showing her the notes and edits, as well as when he logged in and signed out of the call.

"Thanks so much for your help, Mr. Huston," she said.

He nodded as he walked her to the door. "Two blind people..." he said, trying to make sense of it. "Why would someone do that?"

"I'm trying to find that out for myself," she said. "Please do call me if you think of anything that might help," she added, offering him one of her cards.

He took it, waved a slow goodbye, and then closed the door as she made her exit. Mackenzie almost felt like she'd just delivered the news of the murders to family members rather than a kind-hearted young guy who seemed to genuinely care about both of the deceased.

She almost envied that...feeling genuine remorse for strangers. Lately, she had seen the dead as nothing more than corpses— unnamed mounds, ripe with potential clues.

It wasn't the best way to live a life, she knew. She couldn't let the job wipe out her sense of compassion. Or her humanity.

CHAPTER SEVEN

Mackenzie pulled up in front of the Treston Home for the Blind at 11:46, having made better time than her GPS had estimated. Although, when Mackenzie parked in front of the building, she double-checked the address Clarke had given her. The home looked small, no bigger than a casual storefront. It was located on the far west side of the town of Treston, which, while much larger than Stateton, still wasn't much to brag about. While the town was many steps up from the rural squalor of Stateton, it boasted just two stoplights. The only thing that made it the least bit urban was the McDonald's along Main Street.

Confident that she had the right address—which was further proven by the sign that sat in front of the property in a state of disrepair—Mackenzie stepped out of her car and walked up the cracked sidewalk. The front door was separated from the sidewalk by only three concrete stairs that looked as if they had not been swept in years.

She walked inside, stepping into what served as a lobby and waiting area. A woman sat behind a counter along the front wall, speaking on the telephone. The wall behind her was painted a startling shade of white. A dry erase board contained a smattering of notes to her left. Other than that, the wall was plain and featureless.

Mackenzie had to walk up to the counter and stand there, pressed against it and doing her best to suggest that she needed assistance. The woman behind the counter looked horribly annoyed at this and begrudgingly ended her call. She finally looked up at Mackenzie and asked: "Can I help you?"

"I'm here to speak with the manager," she said.

"And you are?"

"Agent Mackenzie White, with the FBI."

The woman paused for a moment, as if she didn't believe Mackenzie. This time it was Mackenzie's turn to give the annoyed look. She flashed her badge and watched as the woman suddenly sprang into action. She picked up the phone, pressed an extension, and spoke briefly with someone. She avoided eye contact with Mackenzie the entire time.

When the woman was done, she finally looked up at Mackenzie again. It was clear that she was embarrassed but Mackenzie did her best not to take too much joy in it.

"Mrs. Talbot will see you right away," the lady said. "Head on back. Her office is the first one you'll come to."

Mackenzie walked through the only other door in the lobby and entered a hallway. The hallway was rather short, containing only three doors. At the end of the hall, a set of double doors were closed. She assumed the residences were behind these doors and hoped the rooms were in much better shape than the rest of the building.

She approached the first floor along the hallway. A nameplate along the side of the doorframe read Gloria Talbot. The door was standing partially open, but Mackenzie still knocked. The door was answered right away by an overweight woman who wore a thick pair of bifocals.

"Agent White, please come on in," Talbot said.

Mackenzie did as she was asked, taking the single seat that sat on the opposite side of the small and cluttered desk.

"I'm going to assume that this is about Kenneth Able's murder?" Talbot asked.

"Yes ma'am, it is," Mackenzie said. "We have another murder in a town about two and a half hours south of here. Another blind person—a member of a home for the blind."

"Two and a half hours away?" Talbot asked. "That's got to be the Wakeman Home for the Blind, right?"

"It is. And the manner in which this victim was killed seemed to be identical to Kenneth Able. I was hoping you could show me around the home, including the closet where his body was found."

"Absolutely," Talbot said. "Come with me."

Talbot led her back out into the hall and then through the double doors Mackenzie had spotted on her way to Talbot's office. They entered a large open space that emptied into what appeared to be a sort of common room. Within the open space, Mackenzie counted eight rooms.

"These," Talbot said, "are the rooms the residents stay in. Unlike Wakeman, we don't have ritzy up-to-date accommodations."

She did not say this apologetically. In fact, Mackenzie thought she heard some venom in Talbot's voice.

"This one," Talbot said, leading Mackenzie to the second door on the right, "was Kenneth's room."

Talbot unlocked the door and they stepped inside. The room smelled of dust and some sort of chemical cleaner that seemed far too strong. Mackenzie did her best not to seem taken aback by the state of the room in comparison to what she had seen at Wakeman.

35

She observed the bed, the small writing desk, the bureau, and the closet door. Everything looked aged, dulled and from another time.

She walked to the closet and opened it. As she looked into the empty space inside, she asked Talbot: "Can you walk me through how the body was discovered?"

"There's another resident here, Margaret Dunwoody," Talbot said. "She and Kenneth joked that they were dating—which is hilarious because Kenneth was thirty-eight and Margaret is pushing sixty. They were always together, having conversations in the common room, eating meals together, and things like that. Anyway, she came to his room in the afternoon to see if he wanted to step out for a bite to eat at McDonald's. When he didn't answer the door, she came inside. She said she knew something was wrong right away. She said the room felt too still. She was freaked out, so she went to the security guard that was here that night—a young guy named Tyrell Price. Tyrell found Kenneth in the closet, dead."

"Strangled, with contusions around his eyes, correct?" Mackenzie asked.

"That's right," Talbot said.

Mackenzie looked into the closet, taking the small Maglite from her belt and shining it inside. She felt around the carpet and the doorframe but found no signs that the killer had left intentional clues. The only thing to be found in the closet was a stray coat hanger, dangling from the tension rod near the top of the frame.

This is a lot more daring than what happened to Ellis Ridgeway, she thought. *Someone actually came into the room to kill him. Which meant someone let him inside. Did they know who he was? Did Kenneth Able know who it was?*

"What's the security like here?" Mackenzie asked.

"Not much to speak of," Talbot said. "There's a single camera outside that films the parking lot, but it's been broken for the last month or so. We have two security guards that rotate shifts on the weekdays. And that's about it."

"Any plans to get that camera fixed?" Mackenzie asked, a little upset.

"Oh yeah. But as you can see, we're not exactly the shining example that Wakeman is. Our budget is a joke and getting that camera fixed will cost upwards of three hundred bucks."

"Is there someone here at all hours of the day?" Mackenzie asked, deciding to let the camera issue go for now.

"Yes. Between myself, two caretakers, the two security guards, and, on occasion, Tori out front, there is always someone here."

"Would there be any way to see who came in and out of the building on the day Kenneth died?"

"No," Talbot said regrettably. "Again...we don't get much money for what we do here. We don't have the good fortune of having generous donors like they have down at Wakeman."

This is the sort of home people are sent to in order to be forgotten, Mackenzie realized sadly.

"Is Tyrell Price working today?" Mackenzie asked.

"No. He's doesn't come in until tomorrow afternoon. Most of the time, our security guys aren't asked to show up until nightfall. Cost-cutting and all."

"I see," Mackenzie said. She was growing irritated with the way this place was run, but she was also starting to feel rather sorry for Gloria Talbot. "How about Margaret, Kenneth's friend? Would I be able to talk to her?"

Before Talbot could reply, a soft chuckling noise made both women jump. Mackenzie turned away from the closet and saw a woman standing by the open door to the room that had once housed Kenneth Able. She was a black woman, thin as a rail with dark black glasses over her eyes. She held a cane in one hand and gripped the door frame with the other.

"My goodness, Margaret," Talbot said. "You scared the crap out of me."

"Good to know," Margaret said. She lifted her head slightly and seemed to sniff at the air. "Who is the newcomer? Who needs to speak with me?"

"Forgive Margaret, please," Talbot said. "When the Lord took her sight, he gave her ninja-like silence when she walks."

"That he did," Margaret said with that same soft chuckle.

"She's also nosy as hell. She has a bad habit of eavesdropping."

"Sure do," Margaret said with a smile.

"I'm Agent Mackenzie White, with the FBI," Mackenzie said. "I'm here to try to figure out who is responsible for Kenneth's death."

Margaret nodded. "I'd like to speak with you, then. I doubt I can help much, but someone needs to be brought to justice for killing that sweet man."

"You good with this?" Mackenzie asked Talbot.

"Absolutely. If you need anything else, I'll be in my office."

Margaret stepped into the room as Talbot took her leave. The older lady then maneuvered herself over to the bed and took a seat.

"FBI, huh?" Margaret asked. "I guess that means it goes further than just Kenneth, right? Did someone else die?"

"Yes. Another blind person, a few hours from here. So if you can help, it would be greatly appreciated. For starters, do you know if Kenneth had been in any sort of arguments with anyone over the last couple of months?"

"Not to my knowledge. He doesn't have any family around here and when he goes out, I'm usually with him."

"What sort of attitude was he in the last time you spoke to him?"

"Well, that was breakfast on the day he died. And he was in a very good mood. He'd just gotten the audiobook for some old George Carlin book. Kenneth was sort of a joker like that. He was cracking jokes and being his usual self."

"Do you think he—"

She was interrupted by the buzzing of her cell phone. She checked the display and saw that it was Ellington.

"I'm sorry, Ms. Dunwoody. I need to take this." She took the call, not bothering to turn away out of politeness. She wasn't sure if it was even necessary when speaking to someone who could not see.

"What's up?" she asked.

"I'm just about tapped out down here," Ellington said. "The coroner's reports show just what we thought—death by strangulation. Tox screens aren't all done yet but based on what we're seeing, they'll most likely be clean. I spoke to a few residents at Wakeman and no one was any help there. A few talked about how much Ellis loved that garden she was found in. Someone else mentioned a recent trip she had taken to a Braille library in Richmond. But in terms of any leads, I'm coming up with nothing. I'm about to head back out to the flower garden in a bit to see if I can turn anything new up, but….yeah. That's where I'm at right now."

"I'm at the Treston Home for the Blind right now," she said. "So far there's very little to report. My meeting with Robbie Huston can confirm that he's not a suspect. And that's it. I'll call you when I'm on my way back."

She ended the call, wishing he was there with her. Suddenly, the idea of driving back to Stateton alone seemed miserable.

"Excuse me," Margaret said. "I wasn't eavesdropping, I promise. I can just hear really well. Most of us can, you know." Again, she gave her soft almost delicate chuckle. "But that man mentioned a Braille library in Richmond, right?"

"Yes, he did," Mackenzie said, impressed.

"Kenneth visited there recently, too," Margaret said.

"He did? Are you certain?"

"Oh yes. He asked me to go, but that's a two-hour ride. Maybe more. And I hate traveling."

"How long ago was this?"

Margaret thought about it for a while and then shrugged. "Maybe a month ago, give or take a few days."

"Was that his first time going?" Mackenzie asked.

"No. I think he'd gone twice before."

"Forgive me if I sound insensitive," Mackenzie said, "but how did he get there?"

Margaret gave that same chuckle of hers again. "That's not insensitive. Just maybe a little silly. We travel the same as anyone else. We have a little van that they'll use to take us to the bus stop in town. Kenneth took the bus to Richmond. From the bus stop, I assume he used a cab. There's all kinds of services on the Internet that help blind folks out with travel arrangements."

"Well, thank you so much for your help," Mackenzie said. "This is very useful."

"Good. Kenneth was really the only friend I had. He didn't deserve what happened to him. I hope you find who did this."

Me too, Mackenzie thought, getting the sinking feeling that this wasn't going to be wrapped up nearly as quickly as McGrath or Langston Ridgeway wanted.

CHAPTER EIGHT

She had come to terms with the fact that a trip to Richmond would compromise the rest of her day. She knew the trips she was taking were necessary, but she couldn't help but feel that her time in the car would have been much better utilized out in the field, actually investigating. Wanting to make the best use of her time, she placed a call to the Braille library in Richmond, letting them know that she was coming and that she'd like to speak with a supervisor or manager when she arrived.

Other than the driving, there was nothing else she could do.

She was in Richmond at 2:49 that afternoon. Her shoulders and backside were sore and tight from all the hurried driving. It was all making her feel as if the day was slipping by while exhausting her at the same time.

The Braille library was in a fairly nice part of the city, far enough from downtown to still be quaint and idyllic, yet with a feeling of safety that was usually present in the better parts of town. The library was a bit larger than she had expected and, as was the norm for libraries, very quiet.

From the central doors in the front of the building, she found herself in the center of a large room. The library itself appeared to only be one room, cut into maze-like aisles by dozens of bookshelves. Several feet ahead of her, situated in the middle of the room, was a counter space that was in the shape of a circle, with a single break in the back to allow the librarians access to the computers that sat there.

Mackenzie approached the desk, identified herself, and waited while one of the librarians paged the manager. As she waited, Mackenzie looked around the place. There were only five others in the library. Three were situated at tables, their hands gliding over the pages of books. At one table, it seemed as if there was a lesson taking place—as if the younger person was learning to read Braille from an instructor.

As she studied this, a rather dashing man with gray hair and wire-rimmed glasses approached her from the back of the library. "Agent White?" he asked.

"Yes, and you are?"

"Sam Batiste," the man said, offering his hand for a shake.

Mackenzie took it and shook. "Where can we talk?" she asked.

"Let's take a table near the back," he said as he led the way.

They parked themselves at the table farthest to the back. As she sat down, Mackenzie was again taken aback at how large the place was. She almost felt guilty for assuming that a Braille library would be much smaller and almost indistinct.

"I have to say," Batiste said, "I've been overseeing this library for the better part of twelve years and this is the first time an FBI agent has come through our doors—well, the first that I know of, anyway. What can I do for you, Agent?"

"I'm investigating the deaths of two blind people," she explained. "Both were killed within the last three weeks. Method of murder looks to be the same in both cases. Both victims resided in homes for the blind. One final similarity that I've just discovered today is that they both visited this library within the last month."

"Oh my God," Batiste said.

"It may seem like a flimsy coincidence, but when you consider that both of the victims lived a considerable distance away, it starts to seem like much more. It's actually pretty relevant."

"Oh, absolutely. What can I do to help?"

"Well, I'd like to have someone check to see if either of the victims checked out any books. I need to find out what other similarities they might share—anything that might link them closer together."

"I can do that. What are their names?"

"Kenneth Able and Ellis Ridgeway."

"Oh no," Batiste said. "You know, I actually remember Mr. Able quite well. I spoke with him for about twenty minutes when he was in here."

"How long ago was that?"

"Three weeks, I'd say. Maybe less."

"Do you recall what he was reading about?"

Batiste smiled at the memory. "Yes. I believe it was *The Lion, the Witch and the Wardrobe.* I don't know if you're aware of this, but this library was created and funded as part of a ministry program. Most of the texts here are religious in nature. Sermons, devotionals, Christian fiction, that sort of thing."

"Did you get any indication that Kenneth might have been troubled during his visits?"

"Well, I don't recall his other visits, so I couldn't say," Batiste answered. "But his visit a few weeks ago gave me the impression that he was mostly happy."

"Was anyone with him when he came in?" Mackenzie asked.

"No. He was by himself. In fact, I helped to make sure he made it to his cab when he left."

"Did anyone else interact with him while he was here?"

"Not that I know of."

"And there's no way to recall the exact date?"

Batiste thought about this for a moment and then got to his feet. "Let me check my calendar and records. I can, at the very least, narrow it down for you. If he checked out a book I can tell you the exact date…but we'll see."

"That would be great. Thank you."

As Batiste left the table, Mackenzie took out her phone and sent a text to Ellington. It read: *Do you have an exact date that Ellis visited the Braille library?*

With that done, she walked over to the nearest book case. Each book's spine was marked with a label with its print title, as well as a bar that provided the title in Braille. The titles she saw reflected what Batiste had told her about the books being religious in nature. She saw titles such as *God in the Hard Times, Understanding the Gospel, Blessings in the Darkness,* and so on. She was broken from her quick study by the buzzing of her cell phone.

It was a response from Ellington: *July 9.*

Today is July twenty-sixth, she thought. *It's been over two weeks since she visited this library. That means that if the killer met Ellis here, he meticulously planned the murder…or had to work up the nerve.*

As she thought about this, Sam Batiste came striding over to her. He looked to be in a bit of a hurry and had the workings of a smile in the corners of his mouth.

"As it turns out," Sam said, "Kenneth Able actually checked a book out that day. Our system shows that it was checked out on the ninth of July."

And there's a connection, she thought.

"Mr. Batiste, is there any way to find out who else was here that day?"

"Sure. We can see how many other books were checked out and get the names."

"That would be helpful. If you don't mind, I'd also like the names of anyone on staff that was here that day as well. Janitors, maintenance, librarians, anything."

Batiste's face went slack for a moment and then a troubled expression took over. "Quentin Neil," Batiste said. "He was working that day. He was fired a little less than two weeks ago—I guess that would have been a few days after Kenneth was here last."

"And why was he fired?"

"He was flirting with a lot of the women that came in. We got complaints that he was taking advantage of their blindness and groping them."

"Do you know if such a complaint was made by Ellis Ridgeway?" she asked.

"I don't think so. We took down the names of the women who made the complaints."

"How long did he work here?"

"About four months," Batiste said. "He was an assistant. Talked about taking training courses but no real ambition to take collegiate classes."

"Do you have an address for Mr. Neil?"

Batiste chuckled nervously. "I have something even better. I can happily tell you that he was arrested just last week for indecent exposure."

"Sounds like a winner," Mackenzie said, not meaning to say it out loud but having it come out all the same. "Well, thank you very much. If I leave my email address with you, can you please send me the list of people that checked out books on July ninth?"

"If you wait about two minutes, I can get it for you now. It'll be a very short list. We don't get many visitors and most of those we *do* get rarely take anything home."

"I'd appreciate that," she said.

As she followed Batiste back to the circulation desk, she sent a text in response to Ellington's previous answer.

Kenneth Able was also at the Braille library on the 9th. Looking into a potential lead.

As she waited for Batiste to produce a list for her, she wondered how things were going for Ellington. *Probably about as productive as things have been for me,* she thought. *With the killer working in such a wide area, there's no telling where he might be. He's almost certainly not at the scene of one of his murders.*

She was broken from her thoughts as Batiste came to the counter of the desk and handed her the list. He was right; it was not long. There were only five names on it, as well as their library numbers and location—in this case, all in Richmond except for Kenneth Able. Nowhere on it did she see Ellis Ridgeway's name.

As she bid farewell to Batiste, her phone buzzed at her again. It was another text from Ellington. *Sounds like pay dirt,* it said. *Do we need to relocate to Richmond?*

It was a decent idea. With the library here, their first real lead, and more resources at their disposal in the form of State PD should the need arise, it made more sense than sweating away cluelessly down in Stateton.

Yes. Can you check us out in Stateton and meet me here? I'll get us a room and send you the details.

Almost instantly, he responded with: *It's a date. I'll fill McGrath in.*

Mackenzie exited the Braille library realizing that she had several avenues to explore with no real direction. *Got to start somewhere,* she thought.

With that, she looked up the number for the City of Richmond Sheriff's Office. It was a little after three in the afternoon but she suddenly felt like her day was truly only getting started.

CHAPTER NINE

Although her afternoon seemed packed, Mackenzie started to feel as if she was falling into a groove. After leaving the library, everything simply seemed to fall into place. Speaking with the sheriff's office on the phone, she found it surprisingly easy to be connected with whom she needed to speak with and setting up a meeting with the recently arrested Quentin Neil.

Due to regulation and policies set in place, certain people needed to be present when she spoke with Neil and because of that, she could not meet with him until 5:30. She sent Ellington the details and he was on board right away.

Rather than get discouraged over the two-hour wait, she set to finding the addresses for as many of the people on Sam Batiste's list as she could—all people who had checked a book out from the Braille library on July ninth. She spent the next two hours meeting with three of those people, all of whom were of no help at all. One, however, did state that she had heard rumors about a creepy librarian who may or may not have grabbed an ass or two between the bookshelves.

She arrived at the prison—more accurately named a *correctional facility*—that sat just outside of the city limits, fifteen minutes early. There, she met with a sheriff's deputy who handed her the necessary forms in order to speak with Neil. She filled them out in her practiced and quick handwriting, as if it was nothing more than a formality.

"I have a list of people who may need protection," she said as she filled out the papers. "I have reason to believe that a man who has so far killed two blind people may have targeted them."

"Blind people?" the deputy asked. "What kind of a monster does something like that? You don't think it's this Neil creep, do you?"

"I don't know for sure yet. But could you maybe have someone periodically run by the addresses on this sheet?" she asked, slipping the addresses she had gotten for the people on Batiste's list. "Consider them a potential target for a killer for the next two days or so."

The deputy nodded. He looked concerned, perhaps thinking that Quentin Neil was more monstrous than he had originally thought—that he might be a killer.

It's doubtful, she thought. *Neil has apparently been behind bars for too long to have killed Ellis Ridgeway. But of course it's a possibility that he'd know who the killer is.*

"I wouldn't put it past him," the deputy said. "You know his crime, right?"

"Indecent exposure?"

"That's putting it mildly. He's been charged with sexual assault, indecent exposure, and attempted rape."

Seems Sam Batiste didn't hear the whole story, Mackenzie thought. "Can you give me the details?"

"Short and sweet…he was intoxicated and jumped a woman in an alley in a busy part of town. Someone on the street saw him punch the woman and by the time someone was there to stop him, he'd pinned her down and was trying to hike up her skirt."

"Who was the woman?"

"A twenty-year-old college girl. A med student at MCV."

Before Mackenzie had time to let this all sink in, a familiar voice spoke up from behind her.

"You starting without me?" Ellington asked.

"Just the paperwork," she said. She really hoped she hid how happy she was to see him—not only from him but from the officer in front of her. "Did you hear the story just now?"

"I did. Sounds like a real charmer."

"He's also been accused of groping blind women at the Braille library—from which he was fired."

"A new low," Ellington said with a disgusted look on his face. "Has to be."

Mackenzie slid the paperwork back to the deputy. The officer took it without looking and led them out of the central waiting area. After ushering them down a log hall, unlocking a gate, and then leading them down a small corridor, he showed them to an interrogation room that resembled a holding cell.

"If you need anything, let me know," the deputy said.

With that, Mackenzie and Ellington stepped into the interrogation room.

Quentin Neil was sitting behind a basic wooden table, small and square. He looked up at them with an almost entertained look, like he was viewing something on television. It was obvious he was not expecting someone who looked like Mackenzie to come walking into the room, though. He didn't ogle her, per se, but he looked a little longer than was necessary.

"This is your first and last warning," Ellington told him. "We know your charges. Look at her like that again and I'll have to have

46

a long awkward talk with my section chief about why I beat the shit out of a no-name pervert in a Virginia prison. Understood?"

"Yeah," Neil said quickly.

The bravado made Mackenzie want to grin but at the same time, there was a part of her that felt almost belittled when Ellington stood up for her in such a way.

"Luckily for you," Mackenzie said, "we're not here to grill you on your current charges. We need to know about the rumors surrounding your dismissal from the Braille library. I hope you understand that based on the reasons for your being here, we're assuming the rumors were true."

Neil looked very embarrassed, almost to the point of weeping. He suddenly found it very hard to look at either of them, staring at the scarred top of the table in front of him instead.

"I'll take that as a yes," Mackenzie said. "Mr. Neil, I'm going to ask you some very easy questions. And if you answer them honestly, this won't take long at all. First question...were you working at the library on July ninth?"

He thought about it for a while and then shook his head. "No. I was out of town."

"You're certain of this?" Ellington asked.

"Yes," Neil said quickly. "About two weeks ago I was on a trip. Up to Manassas. Pretty sure it was the ninth."

"How long were you there?"

"Just a day trip."

"Any proof of this?" Mackenzie asked.

Neil thought for a while and nodded. "You can check with the library. I was at work every weekday for the last few months with the exception of that one day."

"While you were working at the library, did you ever actually speak with any of the women you harassed and took advantage of?"

He shook his head. "No. I thought it might be too risky. It seemed...I don't know. It just seemed dumb."

But groping blind women was perfectly a-okay? Mackenzie wondered angrily.

"Did you ever hear any of them speaking with other librarians or other people visiting the library?" Ellington asked.

"A few times, yes."

"Did you know any of their names?" Mackenzie asked.

Again, Neil went into thinking mode. "One was named Ashley, I think. I'm pretty sure she's the one that figured out it was me and got me fired."

"Do you know of any woman named Ellis Ridgeway?"

"I don't think so," he said. "But...like I said...I didn't know their names."

Alarm bells started to go off in her head. A day trip on the one single day she had asked him about? It seemed too good to be true.

This is him, she thought, feeling a stir of excitement. *This is our killer.*

She studied him for a moment, trying to get a better read on him. She'd seen it several times before—a man fully aware of the heinous things he'd done but feeling helpless and defeated in his inability to escape it. She didn't feel sorry for him at all but thought he might be feeling genuine remorse...just a tad too late, though.

"I think that's all for right now," Mackenzie said. "We'll contact the facility if we have anything else."

She half expected him to give the old tired *I'm really not like this* spiel, but he remained quiet as she and Ellington turned away from him and made their exit.

The deputy was waiting for them by the door. As Ellington closed it behind them, the deputy checked his watch. "That was fast," he said. "You done already?"

"Yes," Mackenzie said. "Thanks again."

When she and Ellington stepped outside, she saw Ellington deep in thought. "You think it's him?" he asked.

"I think there's a damn good chance," she said. "We need to contact Sam Batiste at the Braille library to see if Neil's day trip story checks out. But it seems fishy...too good to be true almost."

"Or, you know...a quick and tidy victory like McGrath and my new best friend Langston Ridgeway hoped for."

She pulled out her phone to place the call to Batiste—to his personal cell number rather than the library, which had closed at five. As she did, the excitement in her gut gave way a bit and let logic come in. As the phone started to ring, a few thoughts occurred to her.

Based on the times of death for Kenneth Able and Ellis Ridgeway, if the library work schedule backs up his story, he's not our guy. Also...this guy is a woman abuser. For him to have killed Kenneth Able just doesn't make sense. And if he was arrested here just a few days ago for a violent crime, I also bet the chances are good of the schedules not lining up.

"Hello?" Batiste said.

"This is Agent White," she said. "I know you aren't at the library, but do you have any sort of software on your home computer where you can pull up the library work schedules?"

"I have it on my laptop. A spreadsheet for the whole year. What do you need?"

"I just spoke with Quentin Neil and he's telling me that he wasn't at work on the ninth of July. Can you confirm that?"

"Absolutely. Give me one moment…"

She waited through a series of noises as the phone was set down, moved, and set down again. She heard him typing something and then, less than a minute later, his voice was back in her ear.

"Ah, he's right," Batiste said. "I remember it now that I'm looking at it. He took the ninth off to go see a brother or sister or something like that. Northern Virginia, I believe. Sorry I didn't make that connection earlier."

She ended the call and sighed. "Okay. So…Quentin Neil was definitely not at the library on the same day that both Kenneth Able and Ellis Ridgeway happened to be there at the same time. It still doesn't take him off the list as the killer, but…"

"Well, yeah it does," Ellington said. "Not that alone, I mean." He showed her the PDF copy of Neil's arrest report, pulled up on his phone. Neil had been arrested on Sunday night and had been in police custody ever since—two days before Ellis Ridgeway had been killed.

"Well shit," Mackenzie said.

Just like that, a promising lead had come crashing down around her. Less than ten minutes ago she was sure she had been looking into the face of the killer and now here she was, back at nothing again.

Suddenly, the packed afternoon that seemed to have been flowing so well for her was coming to an end. And all she had to show for it was an afternoon of fruitless conversations and the knowledge that there was still a killer on the loose.

CHAPTER TEN

It was one of those nights, he thought, where the southern heat fills the countryside like an invisible giant, hell bent on stomping everything. His footfalls on the sidewalk were soft and yet sounded impossibly loud. Even the tree frogs and the crickets sounded loud, almost like some weird fake noise that was pumping through an impossibly loud speaker.

He was walking close to the buildings along the street, trying his best to keep as much of his body away from the sparse streetlights as he could. Dusk had turned to night about half an hour ago, casting the small-town streets into a state of quiet that was almost otherworldly.

But the quiet was the whole reason he was here—well, maybe not the quiet itself but what the quiet brought out.

As he reached the end of the street, he saw the man coming down from the opposite side. His shadow seemed to escort him, stretched out in a fuzzy shape ahead of him by the street lights. He walked with a cane and seemed to be looking slightly to the left where there was nothing more than darkness and the empty two-lane road that ran through the meager little town.

He knew the man's face well. He'd spoken to the man several days ago, reading to him on a park bench just half a mile away from where he currently stood. His name was Wayne Nevins and he had been blind his whole life—all fifty years of it.

He paused in his step, knowing that Wayne would soon be able to sense him—to hear him and maybe even smell him. He was well aware that humans gave off a certain scent when they got excited— a scent that the blind could sometimes pick up on.

Creepy, he thought. *They're like monsters...living in the darkness but able to use their other senses in ways us normal folks will never understand.*

When he thought he had proper control of himself, he started forward again. There was abut thirty feet of space between them— including the spot where the two corners of the sidewalks stopped to allow for an intersection. And it was then, just before he neared the intersection, that his world started to grow fuzzy.

He swallowed down a gasp as he leaned against the building to his left. His vision did this from time to time, growing fuzzy and then swimmy. Sometimes it would fail him altogether, leaving him in a state of absolute darkness for up to ten minutes. It often came with a slight headache as well but he did not feel any pain this time.

And when it happened, he thought of the kitchen in the house he had grown up in. He thought of that cracked and peeling linoleum floor, the sink that always smelled like mildew and his bulk of a mother standing over him, usually screaming about something.

A memory of pain always followed this, but he managed to push it away most of the time.

If he wanted to succeed tonight, he'd need to push that memory away again. If he wanted the haziness to fade, he had to get past those memories…

And just like that, it was gone. That old linoleum floor faded away and he only saw the darkened street ahead of him.

He continued to focus on Wayne Nevins, his darkened shape now hazy around the edges. He couldn't risk losing sight of him or, even worse, alarming him in any way. He blinked his eyes rapidly, as if trying to will the fuzziness away. He hoped it would pass quickly, as it did most of the time. If it lasted longer than thirty seconds, he'd lose sight of Wayne Nevins and also lose his chance.

As he fought against the fading power of his sight, he was bombarded with the usual images that came with the affliction: his mother's leering face, sneering at him and then crying; blood in a sink; his first girlfriend's naked thigh and the elusive, almost mythical area that rested just to the edge of it.

They came like a whirlwind and he felt like he was inside of it. His stomach felt like it had just come off of a roller coaster, ready to eject the last meal he had eaten. He held his breath and fought against it. He knew that blinking repeatedly did nothing to make it stop but he did it anyway. It made him feel like he was at least *trying* to make it stop, like he had some control over it.

Through the flickering images in his mind's eye, he still saw the shape of Wayne Nevins getting closer. For a moment his skewed shape, the darkness of the streets and the play of the streetlights, as well as the fuzziness in his vision, made Wayne look like the figure on the poster for *The Exorcist.*

Such an odd and unexpected thought seemed to halt the flow of memories. They stopped coming, fading out altogether like a blink. Simultaneously, his sight was completely restored.

His heart was hammering in his chest. His mouth felt far too dry. For one terrifying moment, he nearly forgot why he was there.

He looked down the street. There were no cars—there never were after nine o'clock. This town was like any other small shithole in the backwoods of Virginia. The place basically folded up like a blanket after eight o'clock. And the few who were still out and about—mostly teens looking for ways to spend their time and money—were headed to other nearby towns that had more to offer in the way of entertainment and trouble.

With a sense of caution and confidence, he started walking forward.

Ahead of him, Wayne Nevins had slowed in his walk. Wayne had apparently sensed him...perhaps even smelled the fear and excitement wafting off of him.

Not seeing the point in trying to pretend all was well, he stepped away from the building and close to Wayne. As it was now, only the street stood between them, as they currently stood on the curbs of the opposing sidewalks.

"Mr. Nevins?" he asked. "How are you?"

Wayne paused for a moment and then smiled. "Funny seeing you out here at this hour," Wayne said. He chuckled rather humorlessly at his own joke.

"Well, I was heading out for a run," he lied. Maybe his story about running would be a good cover-up for any sort of peculiar smells he was giving off due to the panic of the episode he'd just endured. "But ten minutes into it, I changed my mind. Not really much of a runner."

"Same here," Wayne said, again chuckling at his own joke.

Oh, he's so *got this coming to him,* he thought.

"While I'm out here walking," he said, "would you like some company back to the home?"

Wayne seemed to think about it and then shrugged. "If you're not doing anything else, yeah. That would be nice."

"When's curfew?" he asked.

He was playing dumb. He knew Wayne had to be checked back in no later than ten o'clock. And that was still half an hour away. The home was minutes away, which seemed like a very long distance in the heat of the night.

Wayne was a brave soul, that was for sure. But he had known this about Wayne—he'd known it since the first time he'd met him three months ago. While most blind people were already uncomfortable enough walking by themselves, Wayne did it at night. He claimed it cleared his head, made him more aware of God, especially in the silence of this small town.

He hurried over and fell in beside Wayne. "Lead the way," he said, figuring Wayne would enjoy the dry and obvious humor.

It had worked out perfectly. More perfect that he could have hoped. The route back to the home would take them three blocks north, then two blocks to the west. But they would never head west at all. On the next block, there was an alley they'd be stopping by. And it would be the last place Wayne Nevins ever visited.

"So," Wayne said, feeling ahead of him with his cane. The *tap-tap-tap* sound it made was almost musical. "What will you be reading to me when we wrap up *Slaughterhouse Five*?"

"I don't know yet," he said. "What do you think you'd be in the mood for?"

"Something with a detective. Gunfights. Maybe a sex scene or two."

"I'm sure I can find something," he said as they came to the end of the block. He peered ahead and saw the alley in question, about thirty feet ahead of them.

"I used to listen to *Magnum P.I.* when it was on television," Wayne said with a hint of nostalgia in his voice. "My old man loved it. He did his best to describe what was on the screen during the dialogue."

The alley was coming up. Wayne Nevins had a few moments left to live and he was spending them talking about an '80s television show. There was something profoundly sad about it.

"Did you ever watch that program?" Wayne asked.

"No. I was more of a MacGyver man."

"Ah yes," Wayne said. "I've heard of that show. But I don't think—"

With a final check to make sure there was no traffic—vehicular or pedestrian—he shoved Wayne hard against the side of the building closest to them. Before Wayne could let out a cry, he threw a hard punch. It landed in Wayne's stomach, taking away his wind.

As Wayne fought for breath, he was pushed into the alley. His cane dropped and rattled on the concrete, the only sound to be heard on those hot and silent streets.

CHAPTER ELEVEN

Mackenzie sat up in bed, gasping and clutching at her chest in the wake of yet another nightmare. She was disoriented as she glanced around the room. She'd moved around so much in the course of the last two days that for the first twenty seconds or so of moderate wakefulness, she wasn't sure where she was.

She saw Ellington in bed beside her. He was hogging the covers as he usually did, leaving her naked body mostly exposed.

She kept her eyes on his murky shape as her brain came around. She was in a Sleep Inn hotel in Richmond. In the morning, she and Ellington were going to interview the last two people on the list that Sam Batiste had given her. After that, who knew? It would probably be right back to Stateton to retrace their steps, dig for any desperate interviews, and hope the killer returned to the scene of his freshest kill.

Those plans were overshadowed by the nightmare that had just sprung her awake. The scene had been the same as usual—her parents' bedroom. He father's dead body. Blood everywhere. Only tonight, the bed had also been littered in business cards that read *Barker Antiques.* And every time she had tried to pick one up, it had cut her like a knife. She'd lost her thumb and pinky before she'd given up. She'd turned away from the bed to leave the room only to have her dead father sit up and the bed and scream, *"Quitter!"*

Slowly, she got out of bed. She went into the restroom and filled a plastic cup with cold water from the faucet. She drank it slowly and then returned to bed. The clock on the bedside table read 4:05, and she knew getting back to sleep would be an impossibility at this point.

She grabbed her phone and checked her email. She had a few new ones; several were from Quantico, updating her on past cases and work-related trivialities. But there was another one from Agent Harrison that had the subject line of "Dogs?"

She opened it and read the brief message, surprised that McGrath had Harrison helping her in such a capacity.

A quick heads-up, the email read. *Did some digging into your two victims, Kenneth Able and Ellis Ridgeway. Looks like they both used seeing-eye dogs in the past. Despite the distance between the homes, the dogs came from the same agency. Here's the info. Probably a long shot, but a shot all the same.*

She saw that the address he had provided for the agency was in Petersburg, a town just a little more than half an hour outside of Richmond.

Okay, she thought, setting her phone down and hoping to be able to get at least another hour's worth of sleep. *A seeing-eye dog agency in Petersburg. A busted lead in Lynchburg. A Braille library in Richmond. Deaths in Stateton and Treston. Are we going to venture all over this hot-as-hell state before we get any real answers on this?*

Unable to fall back asleep, she toyed with the idea of waking Ellington up in a particularly exciting way but decided not to. Let him sleep. Besides…she needed to at least rest if she wasn't going to sleep. Even if that rest meant lying in bed restlessly, at least it was something.

Her phone put an end to any hopes of resting when it started ringing at 5:20. She answered it quickly, knowing full well that a call at such a time could be nothing more than bad news.

"Hello?"

"White? Hey, it's Harrison."

"Oh. Hey," she said, not bothering to hide her surprise. "What's up?"

"There's been another murder. Another blind person."

"Where?"

"Right in your neck of the woods. A small town just outside of Richmond called Chesterfield."

We were close, she thought. It was both exciting and disconcerting at the same time.

"Is there a home for the blind there?"

"Yes. I'll send you the information."

"Thanks," she said. "We're on it."

Beside her, Ellington sat up as she ended the call. He gave a yawn and a stretch before saying: "Okay…where are we headed now?"

***

They arrived in Chesterfield at 6:35 a.m., starting the day off with a quick breakfast of coffee and bagels. They parked in the small lot in front of the Mary Denbridge Home in the midst of several police cars. As they got out of the car and flashed their IDs at the policeman in charge, a few others were busy putting up a barrier that would allow no more traffic to pull into the lot.

The officer in charge nodded to them and let out a sigh. "Good to see you," he said. "I just now found out that this is the third murder in a month, is that right?"

"That's right."

The officer shook his head in disbelief. "Come on...I'll take you inside."

"Was the victim killed here?" Mackenzie asked.

"It's starting to look like that's not the case," the officer said. "He was found in an alley about two blocks away, three hours past the mandatory ten o'clock curfew."

He led them inside the home. It was quiet inside, despite the handful of police officers present. Some were speaking among themselves while a few others were speaking to a few of the home's residents.

"The woman you'll want to speak to is currently a sobbing mess, out front with one of my guys trying to soothe her."

"Are there any other caretakers around?" Mackenzie asked.

"Yeah, right there," the officer said, pointing to a woman who was currently speaking to one of the policemen. "Her name is Henrietta Sheldon and she's going to be your best bet right now. Come on, I'll introduce you."

Henrietta Sheldon saw them coming and stepped away from the officer she was in conversation with. Mackenzie again flashed her badge as she approached them.

"Ms. Sheldon, I'm Agent White and this is Agent Ellington. We understand you're the best source of information for right now. Could you spare a minute?"

"Absolutely," she said. Mackenzie could tell right away that Henrietta had skipped the grieving process and had gone straight to anger. "What can I do to help?"

"We've been told that the victim was found in an alleyway and the body wasn't discovered until well after curfew. Do you know where he had been?"

"Well, first of all, *the victim* is Wayne Nevins. And he usually went out for a walk around eight or so on Thursday nights."

"And do you know where he would walk?"

"The same route every time. It's about a two-mile walk that took him by the Baptist church a little ways up the road. Most Thursday nights, their little choir is practicing. He'd walk slowly by so he could hear them singing."

"So you know the exact route?"

"Yes, I think so."

"We'd like for you to take us out there," Ellington said.

"First, though, I'd like to see his room," Mackenzie said. "And what about security cameras? What sort of set-up do you have here?"

"The system itself is a little antiquated, but it works. For what it's worth, some of the police have already looked over the footage of when Wayne left yesterday."

"I'd like to have a look as well, if that's okay," Mackenzie said.

"Sure, right this way."

Mackenzie then found herself being led through the third home for the blind in as many days. This one, the Mary Denbridge Home, was far better than the one she had visited in Treston but not quite a match for the Wakeman Home for the Blind. The early hour felt hectic, as it seemed all of the residents were out and about, milling around with one another and speaking to some of the officers on the scene.

Henrietta led them to a small office-like room beside a much larger office. There were two policemen in the room, sitting at a small table, watching a series of monitors. One officer was manning a small control board, controlling the flow of the scenery on the screens.

"Excuse me, guys," Mackenzie said. She again flashed her badge and introduced herself and Ellington. "Anything of note here?"

"Not that I can tell," said the officer at the controls. "I've been going over it for about an hour now and I can't find a damn thing. I did find where Wayne Nevins left the home and that's right…here," he said, halting the footage. "No one leaves with him. In fact, no one comes in or out of the front door again for over half an hour.

"There's also this shot from the parking lot," he said, pointing to another screen. He played the footage and they watched as Wayne Nevins walked along the edge of the parking lot and then disappeared off of the screen. Mackenzie watched closely and saw no one following him.

"Does anyone else appear in the parking lot after this?"

"No one. The next person you see in the parking lot is the FedEx guy forty minutes later. He dropped off some office supplies."

Mackenzie said nothing, just watched the screens as the officer rewound them both and let them play through, this time in slow motion.

"You're welcome to run the controls," the officer said, scooting his chair back and offering it to her.

"No thank you," she said. "It seems that you've done a thorough job." She then turned to Henrietta Sheldon. "Ready to take that ride with us?"

"Anything it takes to catch this creep," she said.

Again, Mackenzie caught hints of anger and frustration in the caretaker's voice. And second by second, Mackenzie was starting to feel it as well.

***

"What's the family situation like for Mr. Nevins?" Mackenzie asked as they drove out onto the street with Henrietta in tow.

"Both parents deceased. He has a brother that lives in Arkansas, but we've been unable to reach him."

"Are there any residents in the home that you'd consider a close friend to Mr. Nevins?"

"Sadly, no. Wayne kept to himself. He was social and hospitable and nice, I suppose. But he never really participated in group stuff. He'd only been with us for a year and a half. He came from another home for the blind in New York. He requested the transfer because he said New York was just far too busy and hectic for him."

Up ahead, a small Baptist church peeked from around the corner, the soft 7:30 a.m. sunlight seeming to paint its edges. "Is that the church he walked by?" Ellington asked.

"Yes, it is," Henrietta said. "We can park in the lot and I'll lead you down his route if you like."

Not a bad idea, Mackenzie thought as she drove directly toward the little Baptist church.

As they walked out of the lot and started down the city sidewalks, the thrum of morning traffic started to pick up around them. Most were heading into Richmond, heading for work with no idea that there was someone killing blind people in their midst.

While they walked, Mackenzie figured she should test the one connection that the previous two murders seem to have shared. "Ms. Sheldon, do you happen to know if Wayne ever visited the Braille library in Richmond?"

"Oh, most of our residents do," she said. "We house twenty residents and I'd say at least fourteen of them frequent the Braille library. I know for a fact Wayne visited from time to time. I'm fairly certain he had been within the last month or so."

Mackenzie and Ellington shared a look of acknowledgment.

Maybe the killer is using the Braille library as his hunting grounds, she thought. *Maybe that's where he's going to choose his targets. But if so, how the hell do we single him out of the crowd?*

It felt like a weak theory anyway, but she was not quite willing to let go of it just yet. *Maybe I can call Sam Batiste up and have him print off a list of books the victims had checked out recently...*

As that thought found footing in her mind, she spotted two police cars up ahead. There were three cops standing on the street, the lights on their cruisers strobing and flashing.

"That's where he was found," Henrietta said. She took a few more steps and then leaned against the building at the edge of the alley—a small deli that had not yet opened for the day. "And I'm going to stay right here if you don't mind. I can't go in there. The thought of it creeps me out."

Respecting her wishes, Mackenzie and Ellington headed toward the alley. As the eyes of the policemen found them, they both flashed their badges and made a round of introductions. No one offered to help; the policemen simply stepped to the side and let the visiting agents work.

"Where was the body found exactly?" Mackenzie asked over her shoulder.

A younger female cop came over to them and pointed several feet ahead of them, against the wall of the deli. The name plate on her chest read Carter.

"Right there," Carter said. "Sort of half-sitting against the wall from what I understand."

Mackenzie went over to the wall and looked closely at the bricks and the pavement. She saw no signs of blood and no real signs of a struggle. She looked down the short alleyway and saw nothing of significance there. But perhaps the lack of significance was something to be considered in and of itself.

Kenneth Able was found in his closet, in his room, inside the home.

Ellis Ridgeway was found in a public flower garden less than half a mile from the Wakeman Home for the Blind.

And now here's Wayne Nevins, killed just two blocks away from the Mary Denbridge Home.

This guy knows the areas he's working. He maybe even knows the routines and schedules of the victims; it certainly seems that way in the case of Ellis and Wayne. Did the killer know Wayne came out walking to hear the choir at the church? Had he known Ellis frequented the flower garden?

59

Something about all of that felt incomplete. She was missing something.

No sign of a struggle. Not here, not with Ellis and from what we can tell, not with Kenneth, either. In fact, there's a damned good chance Kenneth was killed in his room.

So either the killer is incredibly stealthy...or he knows the victims. More than that, he might be in a position of trust—perhaps the victims did not see him as a threat.

Mackenzie stepped out of the alleyway and looked up and down the street. If her sense of direction was correct, they would return to the home by traveling a few blocks further ahead and then taking a right. She then looked back toward the church. It was currently out of sight but she could easily imagine its proximity to where they were.

Wayne was walking alone, she thought. *Which, for a blind man, is pretty brave. He probably had a cane or walking stick. Maybe a seeing-eye dog.*

She then remembered the email Harrison had sent her concerning the possible lead of the seeing-eye dog agency. And just like that, two ideas occurred to her.

"Officer Carter?"

"Yes?"

"Do you know if a cane or walking stick was recovered from the scene?"

"Yes, there was, actually," Carter said. "A walking stick. I believe the Richmond PD has it right now. Holding on to it as evidence, I'd assume."

"Could you please let me have the number of the person I'd need to speak with in terms of having someone look it over?"

"I can do that. One second, please."

As Carter went to speak to one of the other officers, Ellington came up beside her. She grinned a bit when he placed his hand on the small of her back, realized that he was doing it on the job, and then removed it quickly.

"Why the walking stick?" he asked.

"I think our victims might know the killer. Maybe they even considered him a friend...someone trustworthy."

"You think we might get prints or fibers from the stick?"

"It's a possibility."

"Why don't we just head to the PD to look it over ourselves? Have a talk with the forensics department?"

"Maybe later," she said. "For now, I was thinking we should go see about some dogs."

"Dogs? Is that some weird joke? You know I don't understand your sense of humor."

"No joke," she said. "A potential lead."

"So long as you fill me in on the way, I'm good with that. Also...you know what else you can fill me in on? The dreams you have at night. You were trembling in your sleep last night. Moaning."

She gave him a look that was meant to be sincere but she feared came off a bit defensive. "Sorry," she said. "We aren't there yet."

He nodded and left it at that. "So. Dogs, huh?"

She gave a thin grin and turned away from him as she waited for Carter to come back with the necessary contact information about the walking stick. The silence coming off of Ellington was a heavy one but she didn't let it bother her. Instead, she focused on the handful of possibilities that had already opened up for them this morning and how any of them could lead to apprehending a killer.

CHAPTER TWELVE

They arrived at the seeing-eye dog agency just after 9:00. The place had no name and looked exactly the same as any animal shelter. It was located just off of a state road, surrounded by a small field on one side and an expanse of woodland on the other. It was flanked by a gravel driveway and nothing else, the epitome of an off-the-beaten-path sort of place.

As they got out of the car, Mackenzie could hear a few dogs barking happily somewhere on the other side of the small one-story building. Ellington had called ahead to make sure someone would be there to meet with them; it was a good thing, as the agency was open by appointment only.

Before they even made it to the door, a tall, thin woman met them. She opened the door for them and ushered them in with a smile. As Mackenzie passed her and stepped inside, she caught the scent of dog food on the woman. They entered a small waiting area that contained only four chairs and a small table with a few magazines. Along the front wall, a glass window revealed small office area and, beyond that, without any walls to separate them, a concrete room filled with large kennels.

"Welcome, welcome," the woman said. "My name is Gretchen Slater and I manage the agency. Please…anything I can do to help you with your case, let me know. As you might imagine, this is a new sort of request for us."

"Well, we can't provide you with any deep details of the case, but we're hoping to find some sort of connection between three different blind people, all from Virginia but spread out in distance."

"Well, we do cater to the whole state," Gretchen said. "Parts of West Virginia and North Carolina, too."

"If I gave you three names, how long would it take you to tell me if they've done business here?"

"Maybe a minute," Gretchen said proudly. "Come on back to the office and we'll see what we can find for you."

Gretchen led them through a door and into the cluttered little corner office that was nothing more than a desk and a few chairs shoved against the side of the huge open-floor area that held the kennels and cages. Gretchen took a seat behind the workspace and fired up her laptop.

As they waited for it to boot up, Mackenzie asked: "Do you stay busy or is it sort of a niche business?"

"We stay steady," Gretchen said. "Recently we've started working with service dogs as well. But our biggest draw is seeing-eye dogs."

"Who would contact you about acquiring one?" Ellington asked.

"Usually, it's a caretaker for the blind individual," Gretchen said. "Every now and then we'll get a call from the manager of a home for the blind."

"You ever get any business from Wakeman down in Stateton?" Mackenzie asked.

"Yes indeed," Gretchen said. "A nice place they have down there. Have you been by there, by chance? It's one of the nicest homes for the blind on the entire East Coast."

"Yes, we've been by there," Mackenzie said.

With the computer booted up, Gretchen opened up a program that looked like Excel with a few extra bells and whistles. "All right," she said. "What are those three names?"

"Ellis Ridgeway. Wayne Nevins. Kenneth Able."

Gretchen typed all three names into a search bar and before the results even showed up, Gretchen was nodding. "The name Ellis Ridgeway sounds very familiar," she said. "I think she might have been a resident down at Wakeman."

Mackenzie didn't respond one way or another as the results came up. She saw the results for herself on the screen as Gretchen summed them up for them.

"Here we go," she said. "It looks like only two of them used us in the past. Kenneth Able and Ellis Ridgeway. Right here, though, this little exclamation point by Wayne Nevins indicates that he did reach out and inquire about our services."

"Any idea why he never took it any further?" Mackenzie asked.

"No, we don't keep those sorts of records. But this was, let's see—"

She clicked a few buttons and another column of information popped up. "This was almost nine years ago that Wayne Nevins contacted us. So the information is pretty old anyway."

"Ms. Slater," Ellington said, "how many people do you staff?"

"Just one. I have a guy that comes in and feeds the dogs, makes sure they're all clean and healthy. He just happens to be a damned good trainer, too. Everyone else that comes and goes is a volunteer. We've got some high school kids, an elderly lady that just loves dogs, and the vet that takes care of our dogs doesn't charge for his services."

"Do you think we could talk to your trainer?" Mackenzie asked.

"Oh, that would be easy. He's right out back, about to give the dogs their chow for the day."

Gretchen led them through the rows of kennels. Mackenzie noticed at once that the dogs were all well behaved. A few nipped happily at the doors to their cages while most remained sitting still and silent, cocking their heads in a curious fashion at the newcomers.

When they reached the back of the building, a barn-type door slid open to a small stretch of grass and dirt. About twenty feet behind the agency's central building stood an old building that resembled a barn. The door was open, revealing a musty inside. A man moved around inside, tossing a bag of dog food to the side to get to something else unseen.

Gretchen knocked on the side of the opened door's frame and stepped up onto the slight wooden ramp that led inside. "Hey, Mike," Gretchen said. "Heads up. There are two folks out here that need to speak with you."

An African-American man came out of the shed. He was sweating, wiping away beads of sweat from his forehead. Mackenzie felt for him. It was only 9:15 in the morning and it had to be at least eighty degrees. He eyed Mackenzie and Ellington with a smile and nodded.

"I'd offer to shake your hand," he said. "But I'm sweating a little too much for any sort of contact with people I've never met."

"That's much appreciated," Ellington said.

After a round of quick introductions and showing their badges, the four of them went back inside just to get out of the heat. Mike took a large bucket of dog food with him and started to disperse it into the dogs' cages as Mackenzie and Ellington began to question him.

"So what exactly do you train the dogs to do?" Ellington asked.

"To stay close to their master at all times," Mike said. "I train them to always be on the lookout for anything threatening or unexpected. I can train them to stop at busy intersections and even have them fetch things like canes, shoes, remote controls."

"And you work alone?" Mackenzie asked.

"For the most part, yes. Sometimes some of the high school volunteers that come in here will serve as a decoy blind person just to help the dogs get used to the commands. There was also once a woman from North Carolina that would come in once or twice a year to make sure the dogs didn't have any sort of diseases or were infested with ticks or lice."

"So no suspicious former employees or anything like that?" Ellington asked.

"No," Gretchen said.

"You know," Mike said, dumping some food into a slot in the nearest cage. The Labrador inside the cage waited patiently for the food to drop and then started to eat. "I don't know exactly what sort of details you're looking for. But if you're looking for trouble people that we have had some sort of history with, there's one that comes to mind right away."

"Yes, that sort of information would be very helpful," Mackenzie said.

"There was a guy named Charles King."

"Ah, Jesus," Gretchen said. "I'd managed to put that creep out of my mind."

"Who is Charles King?" Mackenzie asked.

Gretchen and Mike exchanged a look as they tried to decide who would do the talking. In the end, it was Gretchen. She sighed before she began; Mackenzie could tell that simply thinking about the man put her on edge.

"He was a client from about four years ago," she said. "He lived on his own but also had a caretaker that checked in on him. He wasn't one of these guys that was blind from birth. He was in some sort of accident at work and lost his sight—some sort of chemical spill at a factory if I remember correctly. Anyway, his caretaker worked with us. She brought Charles in and he tried out a few of the dogs. One of them bonded with him really quickly."

"Yeah, it was almost like it was meant to be," Mike said with disgust.

"But then we got a call about a month later," Gretchen said. "The caretaker called to let us know that Charles was beating the dog. Apparently he accidentally tripped over the dog's leash one day and lost his mind."

"I went down there," Mike said. "Met up with a local vet and did a surprise check-in. I could have beat the hell out of that man, I tell you. I don't care if he *is* blind. He hadn't been properly feeding the dog. The dog was walking with a limp and was missing two teeth. We removed the dog from the premises and when we got it back to the vet's office, we found a fractured back left leg, two cracked ribs, bruising to the gums, and overall malnutrition."

"We reported him," Gretchen said, "but ultimately, nothing was ever done. He did make some obscene phone calls to us, though. Once we complained about it to the police, he stopped. I assume the cops got to him and warned him."

"Do you think Charles King would be capable of doing those same sorts of things to a human being?" Mackenzie asked.

"Based on some of the things he was saying when he called here, I'd say so," Mike said.

"Do you have an address for him?"

"Yes," Gretchen said. "Somewhere near Lynchburg, I think."

Perfect, Mackenzie thought. *At least it's back along the way to Stateton and not on the other side of the frigging state.*

"If you don't mind my asking," Mike said, "has Charles done something? Something worse than abusing a dog?"

"We don't know," Mackenzie said. "And although I can't give you any details about the case we're working on, we certainly do appreciate your help."

On the way back to the small office space, Mackenzie looked into one of the cages. A golden Lab smiled lazily back at her. Looking at the remarkable dog, she tried to imagine what it must be like to have to rely on an animal to help get from one place to another. Surely there was frustration and a sense of embarrassment at the start of it, right?

What if someone couldn't get over that embarrassment? she wondered. *What if, rather than bonding with the dog and coming to rely on it, the person resented it instead?*

"Here's that address," Gretchen said, handing her a printout.

Mackenzie took it, still smiling back at the Lab.

"I hope you find what you're looking for," Gretchen said. "Feel free to give us another call if you need anything."

Mackenzie nodded her acknowledgment as they made their way back to the primary office area. Outside, it was hot as hell—it felt like the temperature had jumped at least five degrees since they'd met Mike out back in the shed.

"So…Lynchburg?" Ellington said.

"Yeah. Again."

CHAPTER THIRTEEN

"So, let's think about the personality types of the sorts of people we're thinking about," Mackenzie said.

They had left the seeing-eye dog agency less than five minutes ago. Ellington was currently turning onto the four-lane highway that would, about one hundred miles later, lead them into Lynchburg.

"On the one hand," Mackenzie said, "we have a low-life cowardly man that is beating a dog that has been trained to do nothing more than serve people with a disability. On the other hand, we have a man that is driven to kill blind people."

"Yeah…seems like two different types of people," Ellington agreed.

"Exactly. It takes a special kind of coward to beat a dog. But there's at least some sort of courage—albeit skewed and sick—to work your nerve up to murder someone. But at the same time, maybe beating a dog is nothing to someone who would kill blind people. So maybe it's all one and the same. I think it could be a match."

"Another thing I've been wondering," Ellington said, "is why blind people? What would drive someone to target blind people?"

"I've thought about that, too," Mackenzie said. "The easy go-to theory is that someone close to him was either blind or almost blind. Maybe he lost that person and these are revenge murders of a sort."

"Or maybe he's scared of blind people," Ellington said. "Maybe he sees them as a threat somehow."

"Or he could be repulsed by them," she offered. "But again…why? Which leads me back to a family link. You know, if I recall correctly, there was a case from about fifteen years or so ago somewhere out in California where a man beat the hell out of his blind mother—put her into a coma. When he was interrogated he said he did it because his sister had abused him when they were kids. And his mother never *saw* it. He blamed her for allowing it to happen. I wonder if it's something like that at play here."

The conversation carried on like that for about half of the trip to Lynchburg. The great thing about so much time in the car together was that it practically forced them to explore the corners of their relationship that didn't involve them being naked. More than that, it also gave Mackenzie more of an idea of how Ellington's mind worked. And the more she got to see it at work, the more she realized how brilliant he was and what had drawn her to him in the first place.

While the theories started to come to a stop and conversation came in tiny bursts here and there, her mind continued to work over a few other theories. As Ellington closed in on Lynchburg, one in particular seemed to evolve more than any others.

What if it's the opposite of the example I gave Ellington? What if the killer once had someone in his life that was blind and they died? Could he perhaps be killing these people because he feels that he is freeing them from a life of trials and obstacles? Mercy killings, in a sense?

It was all speculation, of course. As of now, there were far too many theories and far too little evidence to back them up.

But hopefully they'd find some hard evidence in Lynchburg. So far, a violent blind person that had apparently beaten a dog in the past certainly seemed like their most promising lead...one that made Mackenzie start to dwell on yet another theory.

What if the killer himself is blind?

***

When they arrived at the address Gretchen had given them, the first word that came to Mackenzie's mind was *squalor*. Even from the outside of the house, she could tell that it would be in miserable shape inside. It was tucked into the downtown area between a house that had clearly been abandoned long ago and another residence where two old black women sat on the porch smoking cigarettes. These women eyed them suspiciously as they climbed the steps to the grimy front porch.

Apparently, Mackenzie and Ellington looked quite different from any other visitors to the area. One of the women said as much with the comment she made before Ellington was able to knock on the door.

"You with the police?" she asked in a high smoky voice.

"No ma'am," Mackenzie said, not giving her too much attention.

"Gov'ment?"

Mackenzie smiled at the way the word was pronounced but said nothing. Ellington remained quiet as well while he finally knocked on the front door.

"Hope so," she said. "I'm pretty damn tired of hearing this asshole scream all the time."

Interested now, Mackenzie looked over toward the women on the neighboring porch. "What sort of screaming?" she asked.

"Like throwing fits. Tantrums. Like he was a mad child or something. Screaming all kind of craziness at all times of the day. You'd think a blind person would be quiet. Just seems weird. He's a strange one."

Ellington knocked again. A few seconds later, Mackenzie heard the sound of shuffling footsteps. "I'm coming already," a voice said, presumably Charles King. "Who the hell is it?"

Ellington stepped close to the door, speaking softly as to not be overheard by anyone else nearby that might hear him. "FBI," he said. "We need to speak to Charles King."

The shuffling footsteps stopped for a moment and then resumed. A few seconds later, Mackenzie heard the rattling of a small chain and then the creaking of hinges as the front door was opened. An older man appeared in the doorway. He looked to be about seventy or so but his disheveled hair and thin stature made him look on the brink of death.

"FBI?" he said, spitting out the three words as if it was some sort of joke.

"Yes sir," Mackenzie said. "We were wondering if you might have a moment to speak with us."

"About what?" he asked.

"You're Charles King, yes?" Ellington said.

"I am." King then looked in the direction of the women on the neighboring stoop, apparently sensing their nosy presence. "Now," he said, keeping his voice low, "what is this about?" he asked again.

"We'd rather discuss it inside," Mackenzie said, doing her best to nod toward the women on the porch without being too obvious.

King was clearly confused, but he sighed and waved them on inside. "Come inside then," he said gruffly.

When the door was closed behind them, Mackenzie saw that she had been right. The place was a mess, with dirty dishes piled up in the sink and clothes scattered here and there. Surprisingly, it did not stink, though. It took her a few moments to spot the fragrance burner in the small hallway as Charles King led them into his small living room.

A radio was playing bluegrass music, punctuated by an underlying hiss of static. Mackenzie watched with admiration as King made his way over to the radio and turned the volume down.

"If you hunted me down, I assume you know I'm blind," King said.

"Yes, we are aware of that fact," Mackenzie said. "And as a matter of fact, that's the primary reason we're here. We're working on a case that involves the murder of three blind people. There seems to be no particular area of interest, though the case led us to Richmond yesterday—the Chesterfield area."

"Someone at the Mary Denbridge home was murdered?" he asked.

"Yes. And they were the third."

King sat down heavily in an old armchair in the corner of the room. "And how has that led you to me?"

"Well, two of the victims had previously used the aid of seeing-eye dogs," Ellington said. "So far that and the fact that they both attended the Braille Circulation Library in Richmond are the only links we have to them. So we visited the agency that provided the dogs to them and your name came up."

Silence filled the room for a moment. Mackenzie watched King's face, slightly fascinated by how he seemed to have a gauge on everything in the room. Blind or not, he was very confident. And she doubted it was just because he was in familiar surroundings. He seemed like the type of man who was not easily intimidated. Perhaps that was why he had opted to not live in a home or have a personal caretaker on hand at all times.

"Would you happen to have any idea why your name might have come up with a local seeing-eye dog agency?" Mackenzie pressed.

"Because I made a stupid mistake several years ago," he said. "I made a stupid mistake and I sort of stewed in it for a while."

"The woman we spoke with said that even after they removed the dog from your care, you continued to harass the agency with crude phone calls."

"I did," King said. "It's not something I'm proud of. I was...hell, I don't know how to explain it."

"Please try."

"I've let myself throw far too many pity parties for myself. Sometimes that backfires and presents itself in anger. Every now and then, it comes in the form of these pitch-black rages. That dog just happened to step out in front of me when I was in one of those moods. That's all there is to it."

"And the harassing phone calls?" Ellington asked.

"I was pissed off that I was in the situation and...wait, look. Are you seriously telling me that you're here because of the dog? You think because I beat a dog once upon a time that I could also be a murderer?"

"We have to explore all options," Mackenzie said. "You just said yourself that you'll slip into rages from time to time."

King waved this off. "It's been forever since I've had one. Years. Maybe it's old age. Maybe after a while you stop caring enough to be mad about things."

A thought then occurred to her—not necessarily about the case itself, but about the psychology of blind people: *Would someone who previously had sight and then lost it be angrier about their condition than someone who was born blind? Mr. King's personality certainly seems to say as much.*

"Mr. King," Mackenzie said. "If we give you a list of dates, do you think you'd be able to provide alibis?"

He laughed nervously and shook his head. "This is insane. And no...I couldn't. But I could give you the number to the woman that comes by here three times a week to check on me. She's sort of a caretaker, but not really. She freelances. But she knows my medical history, knows the medicines I take, cares for me as best she can. She can probably answer whatever bullshit questions you have about where I was when the murders happened, if that's what you're looking for."

"Yes, I'd appreciate that," Mackenzie said, ignoring his annoyance.

"Her card is on the little table in the entryway. I leave it there just in case I keel over while she's away and someone else discovers me."

"Thanks," Mackenzie said, heading in that direction. She waved Ellington over as well, eager to be out of there. The chaos of the place was getting to her and, quite frankly, she felt almost as if she was intruding on this blind man's one safe place.

One thing kept gnawing at her, though. As she made her way to the front door she stopped and turned back to King. "Can I ask you something about your condition?" she asked.

"What?"

"The woman at the agency said she believed you'd lost your sight in a work accident. How old were you when it happened?"

"Thirty-seven. Damn near thirty years ago."

"Do you feel more cheated in that rather than someone who's been born blind?" Mackenzie asked.

A thoughtful look crossed King's face and after a few moments, he shook his head. "No," he said. "At least I have memories of things I've seen. I know what grass looks like, the many shades of blue the sky can be. Those that are born blind will never know that. So no...I'm not greedy, dumb, or naïve. Others have it far worse."

"Thank you," she said.

King nodded, remaining in his seat with that same thoughtful look on his face. There was obvious sadness there, too.

"Let me ask *you* something," he said.

"Of course."

"Why would someone target blind people? That seems sort of cowardly, doesn't it?"

"It does," Mackenzie said.

The simple question from King triggered an idea in her mind, one she had skirted over before but likely deserved more attention.

Yes, it is cowardly, she thought. *Which means the killer is likely scared.*

But of what?

CHAPTER FOURTEEN

Mackenzie felt like a nomad. The case had taken them pretty much all over the humid state of Virginia and without a central base of operations. As she and Ellington parked in a Burger King parking lot, eating lunch and going over their notes, Mackenzie found that she actually longed for the small yet air-conditioned office of Sheriff Clarke back in Stateton.

Still, at the same time, there was something quaint and exciting about working on the run with Ellington. It was the first time she could actually feel a sense of teamwork between them. While the cramped spaces of a car that smelled like burgers and onion rings might not be the best place to work on a case, it added to the sense of urgency.

"I don't know about you," Ellington said as he bit into his burger, "but I'm pretty certain King isn't our guy."

"I don't know," she said. "All that rage…I mean, just because he admits he has had blasts of anger in the past doesn't make him a modern-day saint. I don't know if you noticed or not, but he was sort of a bastard."

"But a blind person doing the killing?" Ellington said. "Seems like a stretch."

He was right. It did seem implausible that the killer was blind. But it also made a sick sort of sense. Which was why Mackenzie was not willing to rule King out so quickly.

A simple phone call will put the matter to rest, she thought. She pulled out the business card they had taken from King's entryway. Ellington watched her as she spoke to the woman on the other end. It took the caretaker a few minutes to align the dates in question but she ended up providing alibis for each date Mackenzie gave her. It took less than seven minutes to clear Charles King.

Back to square one, she thought.

"So the dog link is gone," she said, processing out loud. Ellington knew her well enough to simply nod and speak only when it didn't derail her train of thought. She was aware that his eyes were on her, watching her while she did her best to work things out. Usually, she had no problem slipping into the mind of a killer—but the added detail of blind victims added a whole new level of complexity.

"The Braille library was a link but that died out, too," Ellington pointed out.

"And it might not have been that great of a lead in the first place," she said. "The chances of blind people visiting one of the more popular Braille libraries in the state aren't all that small. It *does*, however, tell us that our victims were book lovers."

"Ellis Ridgeway liked it so much that she had Robbie Huston come in to read to her from time to time," Ellington pointed out.

"Yes," Mackenzie said, then added another thought. "But *who* sent him? He'd have to be part of some agency or campus ministry sort of thing through the college, right?"

Ellington shrugged, prompting Mackenzie to once again go to her phone. She called up Robbie Huston again and he was still very helpful and eager to please. It was a quick conversation: she asked if he was part of an agency that sent volunteers to homes for the blind and he replied in the negative. He was part of a student ministry that worked to serve those disabled in the community—both local and distant. He gave her the name and number of the ministry's manager and they ended the call.

Mackenzie then called the number Robbie gave her—to the manager of a ministry called Servant's Heart.

Someone answered on the fourth ring, just as Mackenzie was convinced she'd be leaving a message.

"Hello?" a woman said.

Very casual, Mackenzie thought. *This really* is *a small ministry. Probably overseen by the college but run by alumni and current students.*

"Hi," Mackenzie said. "I'm looking for someone to speak with about Servant's Heart."

"That would be me," the woman said. "Dori Eaves."

"Ms. Eaves, this is Agent Mackenzie White with the FBI. I'm calling to ask about your volunteer process—how you get volunteers and then how they are sent out." She then went through the brief details of the case and how Robbie had led her to them.

"Well, I can help you out pretty quickly there," Dori said. "We've only had about a dozen or so volunteers over the last year or so. And only four of them are here in town during the summer. The rest are students, gone home for summer vacation."

"Do you know if any of the other three have visited the Wakeman Home for the Blind in the last week or so?"

"No, ma'am. Two of them have been on a mission trip to Nicaragua for the last eight days. The other is here in the office with me today and I can tell you with utmost certainty that she has been here in Lynchburg for at least the last month without leaving. Also,

I'm quite certain she's never even been to Wakeman. She works more with the homeless and veterans rather than the blind."

"I see," Mackenzie said, not liking the feeling of having each of her hopeful questions shot down with such speed and efficiency. On the one hand, it was great to get such fast and accurate information. On the other hand, that was a hell of a lot of Xs against them in such a short period of time.

"Thank you for your time, Mrs. Eaves."

She hung up the phone, looked out of the windshield, and sipped on her soda. The wheels in her head were still turning, but they were getting her nowhere.

"Striking out left and right, aren't we?" Ellington asked.

"Yes," she said. "I have one more call to make. I want to just double-check with the home in Treston to see if they've ever worked with Servant's Heart—the ministry that Robbie Huston is part of. While I do that, can you call the Mary Denbridge Home and ask the same thing?"

"Sure thing," Ellington said, taking a long slurp of his Coke before getting out to prevent cross-talk.

Mackenzie called Treston, and the phone only rang once before Gloria Talbot's voice answered. "Treston Home for the Blind," she said in a dull tone.

"Mrs. Talbot, it's Agent White again. I'm sorry to bother you, but I do have one more quick question for you."

"No problem. What is it?"

"We were led to start looking into a small school ministry in Lynchburg that sends volunteers out to help all sorts of different niches and people in need. It's a ministry called Servant's Heart. Have you ever worked with them?"

"I've never heard of it," she said. "So, no...no help from them."

Mackenzie ended the call, starting to feel rather discouraged. As she thought back over all of the negative responses within the last fifteen minutes or so, she listened to Ellington speaking on the phone outside of the car.

What are the chances this guy is actually part of a volunteer organization, though? she wondered. *If he's smart, he'd know that would create a paper trail. Then again, he'd need some sort of an in if he wants to get into these homes. Maybe there's something in between that we're missing.*

As she pondered this, Ellington got back into the car. "No dice," he said. "While the folks at Mary Denbridge have heard of Servant's Heart, they've never used their services."

"Any reason?"

"Well, it's not state funded. It's all volunteers. The woman I spoke with says they shy away from that due to safety reasons."

Given the nature of this case, maybe that's a wise strategy, Mackenzie thought.

She looked back over to Ellington and, not for the first time, wished she could peek inside of his head. He did not work like she worked. He would dwell on one aspect of a case for hours and hours and then come up with some huge and very effective theory; she, on the other hand, liked to analyze all details in rapid-fire response, assembling each clue and theory like links in a chain being built.

But right now, there was a kink in the chain. She knew she needed to stop for a moment to re-establish her footing. And because the pressure of the case was looming, wearing her down and frustrating her, it felt like the right time to address something completely different.

"Are you still okay with what's going on between us?" she asked.

The question obviously took him by surprise. He paused mid-motion as he was about to eat a handful of French fries. "Why do you ask?"

He didn't give an answer, she thought. But he knew her well enough to know that she wasn't asking out of some kind of insecure female mentality. He wouldn't take the question as the badgering and nagging of some overly attached girlfriend. As such, she knew she could be honest with him without wrecking her credibility.

"It seems like you're pulling away," she said flatly.

He smiled and nodded. "Yeah, I think maybe I *am* pulling away a little. But I tend to do that when I get scared."

"Scared of what?"

He wrestled with finding the right words and then finally shrugged in defeat. "Of having even the slightest part of my life feel like I have no control over it."

"And what are you losing control over?" she asked.

"The way I feel about you. Namely the urge I've had for about a week now to ask you to move in with me."

And just like that, the tables were turned on her. "Is that your way of asking me?" she asked.

"I suppose it is."

She smiled in spite of herself. "I don't know. That's a huge step and I'd have to think about it before I could—"

The phone rang, startling them both.

"Saved by the bell," Ellington said.

"No," she countered. "Just pushing the pause button." She then answered the call with a greeting that sometimes still felt surreal to her. "This is Agent Mackenzie White."

"Agent White, this is Officer Octavia Carter. I met with you this morning at the crime scene. The forensic reports came in for Wayne Nevins's cane. We have a solid print."

CHAPTER FIFTEEN

He was fully aware that it made more sense to strike at night. The lack of light provided an easy advantage. But during the day, no one expected anything. The added bonus that it was just after five o'clock in the afternoon and everyone was in a hurry to get home from work made it that much easier. Also, he knew the woman's schedule like the back of his hand.

He was sitting in the back of a City of Lynchburg transit bus. It had just pulled up in front of a library addition to one of the smaller local colleges. Lynchburg was one of those southern cities tucked just at the base of the Blue Ridge Mountains that hid three colleges in its rustic folds. It wasn't a large city like Richmond but it wasn't small, either.

He sat two rows from the back and watched as the people from the latest stop got on. He knew from scouting things out over the last three weeks that this stop only picked up about a dozen people. Eight of those people were regulars and one of them was the woman he had been following for nearly six months now.

When she sat at the front of the bus, he was not surprised. When she took out her phone, plugged in a set of earbuds, and put them into her ears, he knew her every move. He also knew that when she stepped off of the bus in a while, it would be between 5:47 and 5:50, depending on afternoon traffic.

He also knew that three others would get off at that same stop. From there, he knew every step she would take—and he knew he had a slim window of opportunity in which to act. But he was ready for it. Everything to this point had been absurdly easy. He was starting to think he might have a knack for this sort of thing…that it was something much more than some momentary lapse in his moral reasoning.

The bus shifted into gear with a subtle little jerk and then pulled across the parking lot. He sat in the back, closed his eyes, and waited.

When the third stop brought the bus to a halt thirty-nine minutes later, he opened his eyes. When he did, he felt like another person—a hunter, a killer. It was a part of him he was learning to like quite a bit.

When the bus came to a shuddering stop, he got to his feet. In the front of the bus, the blind woman was standing, holding her cane out in front of her. As always, the middle-aged bus driver helped her down the stairs ahead of the rest of the people getting off at the stop. He waited patiently and when the driver came back up the steps and took his place behind the wheel, all was well.

He started moving forward…a hunter, a killer.

He could feel his pulse, could feel the nerves lighting fire to everything inside of him. He tried to focus solely on that, fearing that his sight might start to waver again. He was taking a risk here…going for someone that he didn't know very well at all. He'd formed relationships with the others, albeit brief ones. But this one…well, this one had simply intrigued him.

She was pretty. She was…well, she was different.

When he stepped off of the bus and onto the sidewalk, he felt like a new man. It was one of the few times in his life when he could see everything clearly, this handful of moments before the kill.

And with that clear sight, he saw the woman about fifty yards ahead of him and it appeared as if she was shining.

He took a deep breath and felt images of that old scarred linoleum floor rising to the surface of his mind.

No, he thought, pushing the command through his body with all of the mental power he could muster.

And just like that, it was gone. Images of his wretched mother would not haunt him this time.

With that assuredness, he started forward with his hands already clenching and ready to work.

***

Cleo Colegrove was pretty sure there was someone following her.

One of the tricks she'd learned as a kid was to walk with soft feet…to almost tiptoe without appearing as if she was doing so. This allowed her to move along at a normal pace while also taking in her surroundings. When she'd got off of the bus, she'd done exactly that; she always did.

Within about five seconds, she'd heard several pairs of footsteps. This was nothing new, as at least seven other people got off at the same stop she disembarked from. But those footsteps usually all dispersed and went their own ways within a block or so.

But there was still one set of footfalls behind hers. Whoever it was, they were keeping their distance.

You're being paranoid, Cleo, she thought. *Who the hell would follow you, anyway? If it's a mugger, they'll be sorely disappointed. And it's not a rapist; even though you can't see yourself you know you're not much to look at. Your mom made sure to tell you that over and over again when you were a kid.*

Still not quite concerned, Cleo continued on her way. She had just come from a class on learning to type on a modified MacBook that had been specifically designed with the blind in mind. She typically caught on quickly to things like that and figured she'd have it down after another class or two. After that, she thought she would probably sign up for another music history class at the community college. She secretly wanted to learn to play piano and maybe one day, when she finally got over the embarrassment of being hindered by her blindness, she'd work up the courage to do so. The MacBook class was really just an excuse to ease herself into the water and—

The footsteps behind her were clearer now. She allowed herself a moment to stop and focus on her surroundings. She knew that she was standing between a little bakery called Rising Grains and an upscale travel agency. She knew these things because her caretaker had helped her with a voice-assisted map of the route she took almost every morning and afternoon from the college. Also, she could smell the phantom traces of the bread from the bakery even though it closed at 3:30 every day. Lastly, she could pinpoint her location with the slight echoes the tapping of her walking stick made as she clicked it against the sidewalk.

From her current location, she had about two more full blocks to walk before she'd reach her apartment. She could make it in less than five minutes, maybe a bit longer if she got caught at the crosswalk the next block ahead.

Another thought crept into her head and it was this one that made her feel real dread for the first time—a thought that turned a bothersome worry into real fear. It was the realization that the street around her was relatively quiet; there was a lull in traffic between people coming home from work and those who would venture out for dinner or drinks around 6:30 or 7:00.

Two more blocks, she thought. *Even if there is someone stalking me with ill intent, it'll be too close to my apartment. If something bad goes down, surely someone will see and—*

Her thought was broken by a sudden shuffling motion from behind her. She realized what it was within less than a second: the man behind her was now dashing forward, no longer trying to be stealthy.

She broke into a run, something she had never done before. Running while blind was, she assumed, akin to taking a leap of faith off of a cliff and hoping the water waiting below was deep enough to not break your neck. She didn't waste time with her walking stick, hoping her instincts and muscle memory would lead her to her apartment.

It's broad daylight, she thought in a panic. *What the hell is this guy even thinking?*

With that, her fear turned into anger. It was an emotion that Cleo knew well. She had chosen to never be the victim, to never pity herself because of her blindness. What she *had* done through most of her life, though, was feel a lot of anger—at her mother, at the world, at instructors who had the gift of their sight, and God.

She had never played the victim in those situations and she'd be damned if she'd play the part now. She stopped running and stood absolutely rigid. She heard the man closing in on her. She could smell him, punctuated with an almost sour smell she assumed was created by the thrill of his sick little hunt.

He's maybe four strides away, she thought. *Now three...*

She could hear the sharp intake and exhale of his breath. And when she could practically feel him on her, she brought her walking stick up and twisted herself around hard. She aimed her stick slightly upward, thinking it was likely where the man's face was—a difficult task in that she could only guess at his height. She knew she was going to lose her footing because she spun around too fast, but that was okay. As she started to topple, she felt and heard her aluminum walking stick strike something hard. This was followed by a surprised shout of pain.

The man had stopped, probably more shocked than hurt. But Cleo didn't care. She screamed out and swung her stick one more time as she hit the pavement. She hit him again, this time in the leg. It was a weaker blow but it still sent a thrill of satisfaction through her.

But then he was on her. She felt his hands first on her shoulder, then on her breasts. She didn't think there was anything sexual in nature about the attack; he was just looking for an easy way to get to her. His hands finally found her hair and she felt herself being pulled backward.

Cleo screamed again and when she raised her walking stick this time, it was swatted away. She heard it clink and clatter along the sidewalk to her left.

Through the pain in her scalp, her other senses fired off an all cylinders. That's how she was able to hear the approaching engine. Her sense of hearing was far above average so she doubted her attacker even knew someone was headed toward them.

She let out a scream and was not expecting the full-blown punch that seemed to smash open the right side of her face. She felt herself getting dizzy, wondering if she might be losing consciousness.

She tasted blood in her mouth as she listened to that engine noise getting closer and closer.

Apparently, it was now in sight of her attacker. She heard him let out a frustrated *"Dammit!"*

And with that, she felt him release her hair. The back of her head struck pavement and it brought a new and foreign darkness moving toward her. She thought she could almost *see* it as it approached but before she could focus, Cleo Colegrove passed out.

CHAPTER SIXTEEN

By the time Mackenzie and Ellington reached the forensics department in downtown Richmond, the police along with a local detective had already started running the print they had found on Wayne Nevins's walking stick. As they waited for results, Mackenzie looked over the printouts regarding the print, the cane, and the crime scene itself. There were a few photographs included in the file, all of which she pored over while she waited.

She asked the chief of police for a small workspace where she also borrowed a laptop. She signed into her email and started printing off copies of all her own files and photos so she could have a physical copy of everything. Working on the move from town to town was making it a little more difficult than usual to keep a running tab on the people and places that were involved.

Ellington sat on the other side of the small desk within the small workspace, sorting out the documents and highlighting details he found significant.

"I've been thinking," Ellington said. "I think it's safe to say that the killer probably lives in one of these towns he's struck in."

"What makes you say that?" she wondered.

"Just a hunch I have. It seems to fit with the majority of serial killer cases we have on record."

"It does," she said. "Even the most brutal killers in history have usually started in their own backyards. While most of them are smart enough to go elsewhere as to not get easily caught, a few will even keep it all local. But our guy…he has a very specific type of target. And he's having to move all over to find them."

"And there should be something there, right? Some clue that can help us decide where he might try to strike next?"

"Harrison sent me a list of all of the homes for the blind in the state of Virginia as well as assisted living communities that cater to the blind as a secondary venture. There are twenty-two in all. That's a lot of guessing. The bureau has already reached out to each and every one to let them know to be on high alert."

Ellington nodded thoughtfully as he continued to sort through the papers. Behind him, Officer Carter entered the room. She smiled at Mackenzie with the sort of acknowledgment she seemed to get a lot from women wearing a badge. It was a sign that they were of the same brood, a group of women in a force primarily run and operated by men—but they had made it.

"Results are in," Carter said. "And pretty disappointing. The print belonged to his part-time caretaker and, I might add, part-time lover as well. We called and spoke with her. Her alibis check out and she hadn't yet heard about Wayne's death. She took it pretty hard. I'd be fine if I never had to make another call like that one again."

"That's rough," Mackenzie said. "Still, thanks for running with that."

Carter looked as if she was going to say something else but she was cut off by the ringing of Mackenzie's phone. Mackenzie answered it almost apologetically as Carter waited in the doorway.

"This is Agent White," she answered.

"Agent White, this is Sheriff Lyle Denton in Lynchburg, Virginia. Through a pretty weird coincidence, I got your number from Dori Eaves, the woman in charge of Servant's Heart Ministries."

"And what weird coincidence might that be?"

"Well, apparently you're looking for someone that's been killing blind people. Is that right?"

"That's correct."

"Well, I think he might have tried it again. This time in Lynchburg, about an hour and a half ago."

"What do you mean *tried*?"

"Well, this time it was a young lady that might have got the best of him. She's a little bruised up but looks to be okay for the most part. And she really wants to speak with you."

"One second, Sheriff." She then cupped her hand over the mouthpiece and said, "Officer Carter, how long of a drive is it to Lynchburg from here?"

"About two and a half hours. Two if you don't mind speeding and manage to miss the traffic."

Mackenzie removed her hand from the mouthpiece and responded back to Sheriff Denton. "Text me the address of where she is. I'll be there in two hours."

***

Mackenzie and Ellington arrived in Lynchburg just after 8:30, in a rental car that was racking up the miles. They headed directly for Virginia Baptist Hospital, where a blind woman named Cleo Colegrove had been admitted after having been attacked in broad daylight on the street two blocks away from her apartment.

84

After checking in with the local policeman on guard by Cleo's door and getting a quick update from the doctor that was attending to her, they were allowed inside her room. According to the doctor, she had not suffered any major injuries. Cleo would likely need a small amount of dental work and she had needed seven stitches in the back of her head from where she had struck the pavement. She'd also suffered a slight concussion, which was really the only reason she was still in the hospital.

When Mackenzie and Ellington entered her room, Cleo was sitting on the edge of the bed, facing an older woman who was sitting in a visitor's chair. Cleo and the other woman turned at the same time to acknowledge them. Mackenzie once again found herself impressed with the way blind people seemed to sense and know the world in ways sighted people could not.

The left side of Cleo's face was swollen. From the nose down, that side of her face was covered in a purple bruise. Some sort of ointment or cream glistened in the light of the room, recently applied by a nurse or doctor.

"Are you the detectives?" the older woman asked.

"We are," Mackenzie said, taking a moment to introduce themselves to the two women.

"Thanks for coming," the older woman said. "My name is Maggie Reynolds. I'm Cleo's roommate."

"Which is a much more casual way to say *protector* or *caretaker*," Cleo said from her perch on the bed. "But yeah, she's a pretty bad-ass roommate, too."

"Cleo, are you okay to answer a few questions?" Mackenzie asked.

"Absolutely. When I heard there was someone with the FBI looking into a series of murders involving blind people, I wanted to talk to you immediately. I mean…I can't think of anything more deplorable than targeting blind people. What a douchebag."

"Forgive me for the weird line of questioning," Mackenzie said, "but I've never tried getting a statement from a blind person before. Without sight at your disposal, what can you tell us about your attacker?"

"It was a guy. I could tell by the hands. And I'm pretty sure my stick whacked him in the face. If that's right, I'd say he's right at six feet tall. He didn't feel especially strong but he's got a pretty solid punch."

"And did he say anything to you?" Ellington asked.

"No. He only said a single word—*dammit*—and that wasn't until a car started to approach."

"By the way," Maggie said, "I've spoken with the police. The man that did pull to the side of the road to check on Cleo never saw anyone."

"Yeah, he was fast," Cleo said. "I'll give him that much."

"How long have you been making that walk?" Mackenzie asked.

"Off and on for about a year or so. But it's not a long walk. It's just from the bus stop to my apartment. Just three and a half blocks."

"And you've never had an incident before this one?" Ellington asked.

"None. Not even any crude words from people on the street. I usually get asked if I need any help...which is sweet but also sort of irritating after about the hundredth time."

Mackenzie started to feel a whole new level of frustration. Knowing that her witness was lacking sight and unable to have seen anything, she felt like she was shooting in the dark. How was she supposed to ask direct and informative questions?

"Where were you coming from when it occurred?" Mackenzie asked.

"From the community college. I was taking a computer class for the blind."

"She's always taking classes," Maggie said. "She's going to end up with like five degrees and more knowledge than she knows what to do with."

"In the past year or so, have you come into contact with anyone that really unsettled you?" Mackenzie asked. "On the bus, in these classes you take?"

"Not really," Cleo said. "Just the occasional kind-hearted person that takes a little *too* much pity on me."

"That happens a lot?"

"Oh yeah. And that's just from strangers that think I've been blind from birth."

"You aren't?" Mackenzie asked.

"Nope. I was diagnosed with Stargardt disease when I was six. I still don't really know if it was caught too late or if my mother just sort of let it go for too long. She wasn't exactly the best maternal figure. She was on her third husband when I got sick. I started getting faulty vision soon after that and was completely blind by the time I was eight. She finally took me to the doctor somewhere in the middle of all of that but it was too late...and expensive."

She lost her sight as a child, she thought. *Charles King lost his in a work accident. I can't even start to imagine what it must be like*

86

to live a life of blindness knowing full well the things you're missing.

"And have you ever considered living in a home for the blind?" Ellington asked.

"No way. Not my scene. I've known Maggie here since I was little. She used to be a teacher at the school I attended when I went blind."

"I was just a teacher's aide," Maggie corrected.

"She's stuck with me through everything. With her as a roomy, there's no need for one of those homes."

"How about you, Maggie?" Mackenzie asked. "Have you crossed paths with anyone in recent memory that was involved with Cleo in any way that seemed odd or scary to you?"

"None that I know of. But I don't hear about all of the people she meets in these classes, I'm sure."

"Any connections to your mother or any of her former boyfriends or husbands? Ellington tried.

Cleo made a chuffing noise. "No. Not at all."

"Tell me, Cleo…have you ever visited the Braille library in Richmond?"

"No. I'm strictly an audiobook kind of girl. I *have* heard of it, though."

"And have you ever contacted a seeing-eye dog agency?"

"Maggie and I have talked about it, just as another form of companionship," Cleo said. "But no…I haven't pulled the trigger on that yet."

"I see," Mackenzie said, feeling stupid for having made the speedy drive from Richmond to Lynchburg. She was getting negative responses to everything now. She'd appreciate just one *yes* that would lead to more information. Hell…even a *maybe* would give her some hope.

"I just want to ask once more…there's *nothing* more about your attacker that you can recall?"

"No. Just that when I hit him in the face, he let out a scream that sounded sort of like a little girl." She smiled dimly at this but then flinched. Mackenzie assumed it hurt her bruised cheek to do so.

"I'm going to leave my card with Maggie," Mackenzie said. "If you think of anything else that might be of help, please call me right away. No matter what time of the day."

She gave Maggie the card as she and Ellington made their exit. As soon as they started walking toward the elevators, she pulled out her phone to conduct a quick Google search.

"What are you checking on?" Ellington asked her.

"A search for medical causes for blindness," she said. "I'd never thought of a medical angle before. There might be something there that our killer resonates with."

"Like Cleo's Stargardt disease?"

"Maybe. It's worth a shot. We don't have anything else to go on at the moment. It might even be worth pinging Harrison to see if he can find me a few names that are experts in the field that would be willing to talk to us."

They entered the elevator at the end of the hall and when the doors slid closed, Ellington placed an arm around her waist. It was a small gesture, but it meant a lot. It meant that he knew her well enough to know that she was getting frustrated and needed comfort—but a distant and almost obligatory comfort rather than the cloying and suffocating comfort a needy boyfriend might provide when he couldn't fix something.

He wants me to move in with him, she thought out of the blue.

That scared her. That had been unexpected and, if she was honest, quite pleasant.

So why does it terrify me?

It was a good question...but one that would have to wait. The elevator came to a stop and they headed back out to the parking lot, Mackenzie's eyes glued to the glowing screen of her phone in the stifling heat of a summer evening in Virginia.

CHAPTER SEVENTEEN

They stayed the night in Lynchburg and when Mackenzie's head hit the pillow, she felt somewhere far beyond fatigued. She tried to remember a case where she had traveled this much but came up blank. Even when she and Ellington had checked into the room, the night had not been over. They had worked together to place calls with all of the contacts they had accumulated so far: Sheriff Clarke in Stateton, the police chief in Treston, Harrison back in DC, the police contact in Richmond.

But they were all unable to offer any new information. It left Mackenzie feeling exhausted and at a standstill. It was frustrating because when a killer spread out his crimes, history showed that they typically tended to get clumsy and leave clues behind. But that was not the case with this killer. So far there had been no fingerprints—not on the bodies, not on the crime scene, not on any objects left at the scene such as Cleo Colegrove's walking stick.

Both Mackenzie and Ellington were so worn out that the mere idea of doing anything other than sleeping once they were settled in wasn't even an option. As she stripped down and got into bed, she heard Ellington getting into the shower. She drifted off before he was out.

She came awake shortly after midnight to the feel of Ellington's hand on her bare hip. She backed into him, feeling the shape of him against her. His bare chest against her back and his legs against her own told her that he was also naked. She slid against him in a sleepy yet provocative way and things took their natural path.

It was urgent, quick, and passionate. They remained in that position the entire time, spooning and with their bodies pressed tightly together. She didn't realize how badly she'd wanted it until it started. It wasn't some love-fueled lovemaking that would rock their worlds but a physical act of need and frustration, taken out with the help of the other. While she *did* climax and fell back to sleep satisfied, it had not been anything that connected them.

And that was fine with her in the moment. She was simply glad to feel him next to her, equally satisfied, when sleep stole over her again.

She stirred awake for good at 4:55. Over the past year, she had adapted to a sort of internal alarm that woke her up if she slept more than six and a half hours. Because she was such a workaholic, though, that internal alarm had rarely gotten a chance to kick in. But it was waking her up now and she knew she would not be able to get back to sleep.

She showered to further kick herself awake. When she was done and getting dressed, Ellington started to stir.

"Sleep," she said. "I'm going out to get coffee."

"You're spoiling me," he said, his head still buried in the pillow.

She'd spotted a Starbucks two blocks down the street when they had come in last night. She headed in that direction, taking out her phone and checking her email as she did so. She was not at all surprised to find that she had an email from Harrison. He had already compiled a list of doctors for her to speak with concerning medical issues that resulted in blindness. He had started the list with one doctor that was located in Lynchburg.

She had started to wonder why McGrath had sent Harrison out with her only one time before pulling him and pairing her with Ellington. Seeing how well Harrison did with compiling data and research, she thought he might end up being a staple in DC, parked behind a desk and fetching information for agents in the field. He certainly seemed to have a knack for it.

With the list saved to her phone and strong coffee acquired, she headed back to the hotel. When she entered the room, she found Ellington going through a quick morning exercise routine on the floor. He was dressed in only a pair of boxer briefs as he crunched through a series of sit-ups. Usually when she saw him in this sort of undressed state, their bodies were pressed together so she never truly got the chance to appreciate his body. She did so then, though, holding the coffees and watching him finish out his set.

"Oh, don't mind me," she said, setting the coffee down. "You feel free to keep going."

"I need a shower after that," he said, getting to his feet. "You know…if you want to join."

"As tempting as that is, I got a possible lead in my email this morning."

We just had sex last night, she thought with a tired smile. It made her feel sexy. It made her feel wanted—which was something she could still not get used to. And behind it all was the lurking reality of him wanting her to move in with her.

She then told him about the list of doctors Harrison had sent her. While it was still pretty early in the morning, she thought it might be a good idea to try to reach out to the local doctor as soon as possible. With the way the days seemed to be getting away from them, she planned on making use of every single minute. It was almost as if...

It's almost as if the killer is purposefully putting distance between the bodies—like he planned it this way to keep the authorities on the move.

While there was no clear evidence to this motive, it was still something worth taking note of. So she started looking back over the case files as she listened to Ellington get into the shower behind her. She called the local doctor, leaving a message to call her back as soon as possible for a potentially urgent manner.

She sipped her coffee, pored over the case files, and started another day—hopefully a day that would lead them to the killer.

***

Fortunately, the doctor she had contacted kept a prompt and efficient staff. Mackenzie received a phone call at 7:10, just as Ellington was finished getting dressed—another ritual she was able to watch and appreciate without distraction.

She answered the phone on the second ring, her voice energized by the now-empty cup of coffee. "This is Agent White."

"Good morning, Agent White. This is Ben Holcomb. You left a message at my office this morning."

"Yes sir. I'm working a case where we think there might be some sort of link between murder victims and their killer regarding a potential illness that results in blindness. I understand that it's short notice, but I was wondering if you could meet for a bit this morning to go over a few things."

"Well, we don't see patients at my office until eight thirty. If you could make it over before then, I can give you a few minutes."

She ended the call, assured by Dr. Holcomb that his office was no more than twenty minutes away from the hotel so long as they got ahead of morning traffic. Mackenzie and Ellington did just that, grabbing a quick drive-thru breakfast and heading to the center of town to Dr. Holcomb's office.

A receptionist unlocked the door for them when they arrived and led them back to Holcomb's office. Dr. Ben Holcomb was a tall man who looked to be reaching sixty or so. He smiled widely at them as they walked into his office and Mackenzie instantly liked him. She assumed he was the kind of doctor that instantly set children at ease and could quickly calm adults with very real worries on their minds.

"Thanks for meeting with us," Mackenzie said.

"Of course," he said. He was at work behind a laptop and pressed one final button as Mackenzie stepped inside. Behind him, a printer churned out a sheet of paper that fell on top of a thin stack of other papers.

"I took the liberty of printing out a few illnesses that have been known to cause blindness. Some of them I know a great deal about but there are others that are quite rare and I have personally never seen outside of lectures about the topics or at conferences."

He handed the sheet over to Mackenzie and she scanned it quickly. She spotted Stargardt disease among the illnesses, the same one that had eventually led to Cleo Colegrove's blindness.

"So, here's the avenue we're looking into," Mackenzie said. "We have someone who is killing blind people. They are being killed fairly close to their residences—all in or near homes for the blind. Yesterday, a young woman who lost her sight to Stargardt disease was attacked here in Lynchburg. We're pretty certain it was the killer, attempting to net a fourth victim. We currently have no solid leads, no description of the killer, and no real MO to speak of. We can theorize that perhaps the killer may have been hurt by someone who was blind—perhaps a parent or ex-lover. But I'd like to look into the medical aspects, too."

"Such as?"

"Well, if someone the killer cared for once suffered from an illness that brought on blindness, it could open up new leads to look into. For instance, the woman from yesterday lost her sight to a severe case of Stargardt disease when she was young."

"I see," Holcomb said. "Well, looking at the list there, you can see it's not a huge list to choose from. Some of the most common stem from diabetes, which is rather abundant these days. Vision loss is also prevalent in people who have strokes, depending on the severity of the stroke. Severe vision loss is also common in people with very bad thyroid issues."

"Some of these other illnesses on this list," Mackenzie said. "Are they rare or harder to pinpoint in patients?"

"Not necessarily," he said. "However, most of those that I've listed can be stopped before any real vision issues are presented. For instance, I see quite a bit of sarcoidosis in my office—mostly elderly African Americans. When treated properly, the risk of vision loss is a small one. But if they wait to come in and the sarcoidosis has started to affect their central nervous system, there can be drastic damage to their sight. I have personally never seen a case of total blindness from it, but I have read cases where it *has* happened."

Mackenzie finished scanning the list of illnesses, complete with a one- or two-sentence description beside it. With a frown, she handed it over her shoulder to Ellington so he could also study it.

"From the look on your face," said Holcomb, "I haven't been very much help."

"It's hard to tell right now," she said. "While there is certainly no smoking gun on this list, it could come in handy later."

"Could I offer a bit of experience I have seen in my line of work?" Holcomb asked.

"Of course."

"From what I have seen, there is a clear delineation between those who are born blind and those who *become* blind later in life. While I'm sure it is certainly not true for all cases, there seems to be more hostility and negativity from those who have lost their sight later in life. Those who are born with it learn to adapt rather young and sort of learn to grow with it. I assume you've considered that the man you're looking for might have vision issues of his own?"

"We have," Mackenzie said, wondering if the killer might be afflicted by one of the illnesses on the list Holcomb had given them. "But it's good to know that I can now back that theory up with the educated opinion of an eye doctor. Thank you, Dr. Holcomb."

With that, Mackenzie and Ellington took their leave. On the way to the car, Mackenzie continued to think about a killer who might have vision problems. Might that be what was spurring him on?

Maybe the very existence of blind people terrifies him because it's the end result of what he fears he could be, she thought. *Maybe his vision gave out on him when he was after Cleo Colegrove and that's how she was able to escape…*

"That was sort of eye-opening," Ellington said. "I knew there were a few disorders and sicknesses that could screw with your vision, but I didn't know the list was so long. Maybe our guy suffers from something on Holcomb's list."

"It's a possibility," Mackenzie said. She took a picture of the list with her phone and sent it via text to Harrison. She followed up with a message that read: *Can you check to see if any of our victims suffered from any of these conditions? Also check medical records within the state of Virginia to see if any patients presented with these conditions and were flagged by the doctors due to behavior or psychological instability. Long shot but it could help.*

"I think we should head back to the Mary Denbridge Home," Ellington suggested as he started the car. "It's the closest scene to us and we didn't really get to speak to any of the other residents.

Maybe they saw something...ah hell...not *saw*...you know what I mean."

"I was thinking the same thing," she said. "But I'm leaning more toward heading back to Stateton, to the Wakeman Home. I don't know why; I know the Denbridge home is more recent but the thing with Wakeman seems bigger somehow. There's a lot of state money tied up there and I'd think there might be some answers wrapped up in a paper trail. We just need to know where to start the trail."

"Why would that help?" Ellington asked. "What kind of paper trail would lead us to the killer?"

"I'm pretty certain the killer knows the victims in some capacity or another. He had to know them. I'd bet you anything that the killer has stepped foot inside each and every one of these homes. And his presence is the freshest there."

"So you want to head back to the sticks?" Ellington asked, joking but clearly a little disgruntled. "In the midst of all of this heat?"

"We can check your theory first," she said. "Couldn't hurt."

"Gee, thanks," he said. "One other quick thing first, though."

Before she could say *What?* he was leaning over the armrest. He took the side of her face in his hands and kissed her. It started slow but evolved into something laced with their usual heat and chemistry. When he pulled away, she was a bit light-headed.

She was so out of sorts that when her phone buzzed in her pocket, it startled her more than it should have. A little embarrassed, she reached for it and took it out. Harrison's name was on the display.

"I texted you like five minutes ago," she said. "If you already have results for me, you're a magician."

"Well, send me my Hogwarts letter...I got a hit for you."

She snickered a bit at the joke. She thought very hard about whether or not she had ever heard Harrison tell an actual joke before.

"Turns out you had it under your nose from the start," Harrison said. "I've got a man who lives in a little place called Randolph, Virginia. It's about fifteen miles west of Stateton. His diabetes went untreated for a little too long and not only did he nearly die back in 2011, he officially lost about eighty percent of his eyesight last year. I've called over for a complete set of medical records to be emailed to you."

"That's a great match, Harrison."

"Oh…it gets better. Before Wakeman went through its major upgrade, it was a much smaller place. And this gentleman just happened to be a caretaker—a caretaker that was fired for an alleged sexual relationship with one of the residents."

"Sounds like a jackpot to me," she said, her heart already hammering in her chest.

"I thought so, too. I'll shoot you his name and address as well."

"So we're headed back to Stateton," she said dryly. "Thanks a ton, Harrison."

When she ended the call, Ellington was looking at her, eyes raised and his mouth cast in a frown. "Shit. You were right, huh?"

"You said it, not me," she said. "To Stateton, please."

CHAPTER EIGHTEEN

When they arrived back at the police headquarters in Stateton, Mackenzie found that she was actually quite glad to see Sheriff Clarke. Maybe it was just his familiar face in the midst of a group of days that had introduced them to countless faces that, in the end, had been very little help. She'd called ahead as a courtesy to let Clarke know that they'd be going after a guy who seemed to fit the profile—a guy who was in Clarke's own backyard and within his jurisdiction by about three miles of the county line.

Clarke met them in front of the police station when they pulled up at 10:05. He was smoking a cigarette and drinking coffee. He wasted no time when Ellington pulled up. He waved them over toward his patrol car, opening the passenger side door for Mackenzie.

Look at that, she thought. *An actual display of the southern hospitality I've always heard so much about.*

"I won't lie to you," Clarke said. "I'm not too thrilled about what we're about to do."

"You said you knew him when we spoke on the phone," Mackenzie said. "How well do you know him?"

"Lenny Peters," Clarke said with a heavy sigh in his voice. "Everyone knows him well enough around here, I guess. He's got to be about sixty by now, I'd guess...a little older than me. He was a good man from what everyone knew. But then he got sick and all of this nasty business came out about him."

"You mean the sexual misconduct with a Wakeman resident?" Ellington said from his place in the back seat.

Clarke had pulled the patrol car out onto the two-lane road, now glancing back at Ellington in the rearview mirror.

"Yeah, that's what. But that was only the tip of the iceberg. Once that story came out—a story that was never proven, by the way—two more women spoke out about sexual advances. One of them happened to be a young lady that said Lenny had sex with her when she was fourteen and Lenny was forty-seven. *That* story just happened to be true. Evidence and everything. So after that story was proven, everyone assumed the Wakeman story was, too."

"Was it assault?"

"No, just groping. Nothing violent from what I gather. It's hard for me to fathom, you know? It's a small town. Hell...a small *county.* And I knew Lenny. I would have never suspected anything like that out of him. But I was the one that had to arrest him when that woman came forward about the underage sex. Of course, it doesn't matter that it was consensual. She was fourteen and that's that.

"Anyway...I think maybe the stress of it all caught up to him. His diabetes led to him losing his sight. I don't think he's blind, but he might as well be from the way I hear it. I feel bad for the man, I really do. Yeah, sleeping with a girl that young is nasty and uncalled for but that was his sin, you know? It was done. And now he's been reduced to an overweight man that can barely see, living off of welfare and with a pretty bad drinking habit. He's become a ghost."

"When's the last time you spoke to him?" Mackenzie asked.

"When I arrested him. I've seen him on the road here and there and we'll wave. But that's about it. But look...yeah, sleeping with a young girl is one thing. But I'll buy you and all your DC friends a round of drinks if Lenny Peters killed someone."

"Why is that?"

"He's gone to shit. He stopped caring for himself. It would be hard for him to be sneaky. I guess you'll see for yourself when we get to his place."

Clarke left it at that. There was a stern sort of look on his face as he stared ahead through the windshield. Mackenzie wasn't sure if he was upset by the fact that he was going to have to question a local man that he pitied about the murders or that a possible suspect might have been right under his thumb the whole time. Whatever it was, she left him to his silence as he continued to maneuver them through the thin country roads while the day grew hotter outside.

**

Lenny Peters lived in a mobile home on what felt to Mackenzie like a lonely stretch of land tucked about a quarter of a mile off of the main road. His driveway was nothing but a dirt track that came to a stop in an overgrown yard. The home itself was what Mackenzie thought of as a stereotypical southern lower-class abode. While it was not sitting on concrete blocks or struts, the front porch looked like it might fall over if nudged the wrong way. Several empty beer bottles were scattered on the porch and a long-dead potted plant was overturned.

Clarke led them up the rickety porch steps and knocked on the aluminum screen door. The sound it made had Mackenzie taking a step back; it was loud and hollow and made it sound as if the trailer might fall down right in front of them. After a few seconds, they could hear a response from inside, a thundering sort of motion that she assumed was footsteps headed for the door.

When the door was answered, the interior wooden door flimsily swinging open to reveal the inside of the trailer, a large black man stood before them. He was easily two hundred and fifty pounds—and that was being generous. When he turned his head slowly to look at the three people on his porch, the way his neck and stomach revealed more folds of flesh made Mackenzie think he might be closer to three hundred pounds.

"Robert," Lenny Peters said with an aggravated tone. "Who are these people?"

"Hey yourself, Lenny. How are you?" Clarke asked, trying to avoid Lenny's instant paranoia.

"I'm the same as I have been for the past couple of years. Fat, sick, and my damned eyes stop working every now and then."

"That's actually why these people are here with me," Clarke said.

"I'm Agent White," Mackenzie said, stepping forward. "And this is my partner, Agent Ellington. We're with the FBI, in town investigating a murder."

"Ellis Ridgeway, right?" Lenny said.

"That's right," Mackenzie said skeptically.

"It made the local paper yesterday," Clarke said apologetically. "It's all over town now. People are all up in arms about it."

"So why are you here at my house if Ellis Ridgeway was killed?" Lenny asked.

"Can we come inside to speak about it?" Ellington asked.

"No. We're fine out here on the porch."

With that, Lenny stepped forward and out into the porch. When his added weight stood upon the boards, she could feel the whole porch sway a bit. Her legs steadied themselves and her muscles were prepared to jump if necessary. When he closed the door behind him, she caught a peek inside and was relieved that they wouldn't be heading inside. She was fairly certain that he was denying them access to his home not because of any sort of guilt or something to hide—but because it was a mess. She saw a living room with several plates on the floor, countless empty beer cans and bottles, and a stack of magazines that was at least a foot tall, some of which had fallen over into the floor. To say that Lenny Peters lived in squalor was putting it lightly.

"We're here, quite frankly," Mackenzie said, "because your current condition makes you something of a suspect. Though—"

She could get no further, though. Lenny started to cackle, a deep belly laugh that was somewhere between a wheeze and a bark. "Ha! That's me, all right. A sneaky, stealthy killer!" He then stopped laughing and looked Mackenzie straight in her eyes. "Bitch, look at me. You think I've got the kind of body to sneak around in hiding and killing people?"

"Whoa, Lenny," Clarke said. "Look, I realize it's a dumb accusation, too. But this is a federal agent. Call her names again and I can slap the cuffs on you."

Lenny Peters shook his head at this remark, as if it were ridiculous. "Okay. My bad. So…you think I'm a killer, huh?"

The hell of it was that she was certain he was *not* the killer. He had been right; the idea of someone his shape, size, age, and in his condition successfully eluding crime scenes quickly and leaving no evidence behind was preposterous.

"Mr. Peters, are you currently employed?" she asked.

"No."

"So I take it you have some sort of government assistance to help get you by?"

"That and some money I got from selling some real estate a few years back when I got out of jail. Not that it's any of your business. I do small engine repair, too. Mowers and things like that."

"If you don't mind my asking…how often does your vision start to go out?"

He shrugged and suddenly seemed tired. He no longer seemed offended that he'd been bothered by FBI agents over a crime he most certainly did not commit, but he did seem a little flustered.

"Maybe three times a week. It got better for a while there. But…my body's all old and tired and fat."

"You can get better," Clarke said, as if he thought he needed to provide a local flair of support and encouragement.

Lenny gave another of his throaty chuckles and nodded. "Yeah, I could. But every doctor I've been to makes it sound like too much damn work. And it might be too late, anyway."

He's given up, Mackenzie thought. *That's why he lives in this run-down trailer among piles of filth and garbage. That's why he drinks so much. He's given up on life—and that sort of lack of motivation isn't characteristic of a murderer.*

Mackenzie nodded and looked him in his eyes, doing what she could to help Lenny feel important and needed. "Thank you, Mr. Peters. But I think we're done here."

"Don't think I'm a killer anymore?" he said with a sad little smile.

"No, I don't."

"I hope you catch the asshole," he said. "Someone that could kill a woman as sweet as Ellis Ridgeway needs to be hung by a rope."

"Did you know her?" Ellington asked.

"No. But my brother is friends with another woman at Wakeman that was friends with Ellis. Nina Brady, I think her name is."

"That'd be her," Clarke said, heading down the stairs and clearly glad to be done with this detail. "She's up there in age, but is almost like a mother to the residents in that place."

Mackenzie nodded, knowing where their next stop would be—back to Wakeman. She gave a cursory nod to Lenny as she made her way down the stairs. "Thanks again, Mr. Peters."

The two agents and the local sheriff walked down the porch stairs and back to their car. As Mackenzie slid into the passenger seat, she watched Lenny walk back into his house. Just watching the man move through his doorway was disheartening. His posture alone indicated that the man had given up on just about everything. Mackenzie wondered what sort of meds he was on and, beyond that, if he was even taking them.

As Clarke drove them back down the dirt road and back toward the main highway, his cell phone rang. He answered it gruffly, clearly a man who hated such conveniences, and Mackenzie listened to one side of a very short and apparently aggravating conversation.

After only two curt responses, Clarke hung up and tossed the phone up onto the dashboard. "Shit," he said.

"Something wrong?" Mackenzie asked.

He grinned and shook his head. "Looks like you came back at the right time," he said. "We've got some trouble down at the station."

CHAPTER NINETEEN

When Clarke had said *trouble at the station,* Mackenzie's mind had conjured up the sort of chaotic circus she sometimes saw in DC when things got out of hand or a case had finally been clutched by the media. So when they arrived at the Stateton PD and she saw only a handful of cars and a single news van, she was relieved.

For a while.

They got out of the car and headed for the front doors only to be accosted by a single news reporter and a camera man who looked like he'd just come straight out of college. Mackenzie did her best to ignore the short female reporter, looking past her and to the doors of the PD. She saw a few people huddled there, peering out. Among them was a man she'd had the displeasure of meeting for about ten minutes several days before: Langston Ridgeway.

I'd assume he's the source of the trouble, she thought.

Mackenzie barreled past the reporter without a word as Ellington trailed behind. As they reached the doors, she heard Clarke giving in to the reporter; he did not offer any information, however, but a rather rude dismissal that Mackenzie was sure would be all over the local news within an hour or so.

As she neared the door, another man she'd briefly met a few days before opened the door for her. Officer Lambert smiled at her briefly as she stepped inside. She returned it, but her eyes were on Langston Ridgeway. She felt the urge to say something to him but never got the chance. Behind her, Clarke seemed to explode through the doors, wedging between Mackenzie and Ellington to get right in Ridgeway's face.

"Is this your doing, you little weasel?" Clarke said. "I know you're used to getting everything handed to you, so you felt you had to get the media to step in to help you get what you wanted this time?"

"How dare you!" Ridgeway was indignant, though Mackenzie was pretty sure some if it was an act, pure and simple. "My mother is dead and you've got no results. Even these rejects from Washington haven't been able to find her."

"That's true," Mackenzie said, placing a reassuring hand on Clarke's shoulder and gently pulling him back before he did something he would later regret. She then took his place, standing toe-to-toe with Ridgeway. "But what you don't realize by trying to use the media to get what you want, is that when the media gets involved, it hinders our work. So it makes me wonder if this is just some glorified PR campaign for your next little voting event. Because it sure as hell isn't going to do anything to help find your mother's killer.'

"How dare you speak to me like th—"

"I'm out of DC," she said. "Your little power of position is nothing new to me. I see it every day. You don't impress me. So if you truly want us to find your mother's killer, you should keep your mouth shut and stop whining to the news outlets."

Ridgeway looked like a cornered animal. It was clear that he was not accustomed to people talking to him in such a way.

"Your supervisor will hear about this!"

Ellington laughed slightly behind Mackenzie. He then pulled out his wallet, took out a business card, and tossed it gingerly at Ridgeway. It hit his chest and then fluttered to the floor. "That's his business card. Make sure to tell him I said hello."

Ridgeway looked as if he'd been slapped in the face. His shock was nearly comical. He looked around the room, realizing for the first time that there was no one there to back him up.

"Now," Clarke said, "kindly get the hell out of my station before I arrest you for interfering in a case. I bet the camera man and reporter outside would *love* to see that."

Ridgeway looked like he might scream or cry or both at any moment. "You haven't heard the last of this. Mark my word."

"Consider it marked," Clarke said. "Now get out."

Ridgeway did as he was asked, though not before giving all three of them venomous stares. When he made his way out the doors, he seemed more than happy to stop and have a chat with the news anchor.

"I guess that could have been handled better," Clarke said, hands on his hips and looking back toward his office.

"You have to put it out of your mind for now," Mackenzie said. "I know that's easier said than done, but all it does is distract you. We need to keep working toward results."

Clarke nodded. "Yeah. Now…if we could just find some…."

"Well, I think I'd like to head back to Wakeman," she said. "If this woman Lenny mentioned was close to Ellis, maybe she can give us some clue or lead we've somehow managed to overlook."

"Nina Brady," he said. "If you want to speak to her, I can make the call to the home and let them know you're on the way."

"That would be appreciated."

With a slump in his shoulders and obvious irritation on his face, Clarke headed down the hall. "Let me know if you need anything out of me or my men," he called out over his shoulder.

As Mackenzie and Ellington headed back outside, she saw that Langston Ridgeway was getting back into his car. The two-piece news crew saw them coming back out and headed their way. But all it took was a stern look and shake of the head from Mackenzie to make then turn on their heel, back toward the little news van at the far end of the parking lot.

"You okay?" Mackenzie asked Ellington as they got into the car.

"Yeah, why?"

"The little scene with the business card....that was funny but not at all like you."

Ellington shrugged and sighed. "I don't know. Little whiny politicians like that get on my nerves. The small-town ones in particular are the worst."

"Sounds like you have some experience in that area."

"I do, unfortunately. Where I grew up...it was awful." He then seemed to think about something as he started the car. "You know, you and I don't really share stuff like that. Do you think we should?"

A brief flare of panic soared up in Mackenzie and she wasn't quite sure why. She only shrugged as Ellington pulled out of the lot and onto the road.

"I'm going to assume if something like that makes you uneasy," he said, "then I probably scared the hell out of you with this whole moving in thing, huh?"

The sad thing was that he was right. It *had* scared her—and the thought of it still scared her.

"Look, I'm sorry," he said. "Sure, maybe it was a little over the top and sudden, but it was what I was feeling. It's what I've *been* feeling for a few weeks now. It's scary as hell to me...but well, there it is."

They were back on the road now, headed to Wakeman. She appreciated his vulnerability but there was something about seeing him so animated and exposed that also scared her. It was, she supposed, what caused her to say the first thing that came to her heart.

"We can't live together," she said. "If we're being honest, the romance between us is already molding the way we work together. I know it is for me, anyway. It makes me feel irresponsible—like I'm putting the job second."

"Yeah, but I think we—"

"It's a bad idea," she said, a little coldly. And then, to add insult to injury, she continued with: "And I'd like that to be the end of it for now. We have a case that's kicking our ass and I'd like to put all of my attention on that for right now."

"Got it," Ellington said, the word coming out of his mouth like a bullet. He then cast his eyes on the road ahead, unblinking. His brow was furrowed and he was clearly upset but he remained silent.

To avoid making matters worse, Mackenzie did the same.

CHAPTER TWENTY

Today's book was another one that he personally loved. He'd read it to himself at least a dozen times and although it was technically a children's book, it had a certain charm to it that resonated with anyone—especially someone dealing with health scares or some sort of physical disability.

He read from *Tuck Everlasting* as if he were a pastor reading Scripture. He felt each word on his tongue and expressed it with care. He could not escape the weight the story carried in his life. It was what his mother had read to him after that terrible day—the day he had lain on the linoleum kitchen floor, sure that he would die and thinking the pain would never end.

She'd done everything she could to compensate for it—for about a year or so anyway. After that, the bitch had just given up and resorted back to her old ways of abuse.

But now, reading the book as a grown man, it was more like his story. He could pretend his mother had never read it to him and that he was discovering it for himself.

In front of him, sitting in the cushioned rocking chair, the blind woman smiled. He smiled back, although she could not see, between sentences. Something about the way they relied on him was, at its heart, sweet. They could easily be renting or downloading audiobooks and listening to them on their own time. But he knew that something about the human interaction aspect of it was really why they asked him to read to them. A live and in-person human voice carried a certain weight and charisma that an audio recording could not, no matter how good the narrator was.

Truthfully, something about the process calmed him. It set him at ease, which was not something that happened easily. After the way his last few days had gone, he needed this sense of calm, this sense of being refocused.

The woman in Lynchburg had gotten away from him. His damned vision had nearly given out on him, sidetracking him long enough in his attempt to take Cleo Colegrove down. Even after he'd felt that nearly killer-like instinct wash over him, his vision had failed him…just like it had done ever since that day his mother had hurt him so badly.

Sometimes he still felt the heat of the burner on the stove.

Sometimes he still felt the burning of his own flesh.

All of that had tried rushing up on him as he had tracked down Cleo Colegrove but he had managed to somehow not let it incapacitate him. In the end, that's what had caused her to get away from him. And he was not going to let that happen again.

He'd kept his eyes on the news from that area and the story had gotten little more than a mention on the evening and late night news, each story ending with the subjective statement: *an investigation is ongoing.* He had not yet seen any story linking the attack to the murders of three blind people throughout the state.

He did not fear the day when the connection was made. He simply wanted to know when the pressure was being applied. And so far, either a link had not been made or the authorities were choosing to keep it quiet.

He figured the murders would all come to light soon enough, placed on television, linked together, and made a big deal of. He wasn't sure what he'd do at that point but figured there was no sense in worrying about that just yet.

So for now, he'd just focus on his next task—a forty-nine-year-old woman named Dana Polson. This was his first time reading to her and her caretaker seemed to really like him. He was sitting in what he guessed most people would call a parlor, sitting on a couch and reading *Tuck Everlasting.* The caretaker, an old woman who had been helping the blind since she was a twenty-five-year-old straight out of college and looking for opportunities to volunteer in social work, was somewhere else in the house.

Dana had lived alone for the last three years, tiring of the community within the assisted living home she'd lived in for so long.

This one, too, was closer to him. No more driving and chasing down his subjects (although that had been fun and challenging). He figured he'd kill Dana and by the time her body was discovered, he'd be somewhere else. Maybe back at Treston, since their security was such a joke. And besides that…there were at least two others there he wanted to kill.

He wasn't sure what it was that called to him from those people. He knew they could not see, but he felt that they could see *him.* More than that…he had lived in their shoes for about four months of his childhood. He knew about that special darkness, the world of the blind. He'd lived in it after his mother had burned his face on the stove, totally ruining his left eye.

His entire vision had gone out for four months and had inexplicably come back in his right eye. He'd later been given a glass eye when he could afford it—his mother had certainly not paid for it, that was for sure.

And now, with his often faulty vision that seemed to come and go when it pleased, he saw his victims in a whole new way. When he had been there, in that darkness that only the blind know so intimately, he had understood it all. The blind *could* see. They could see better than most sighted people. They could see *into people*—oh yes.

And some of them saw into him. They saw the ugliness inside of him. They saw what he had done in the past—to his girlfriends and his mother.

And no one could know those secrets.

Dana Polson saw it. Of course, like the others, she was not judging him for it. He knew she saw all sorts of evil in people. His sins were minor compared to others. But still…he could not live his life with others knowing what he had done. It was too shameful.

Yes, Dana knew. And while it might be a while before he dispatched her, he knew she would say nothing about what she saw in him. None of them ever did.

And that was fine with him. His mishap the other night was telling him fairly plainly that he needed to slow down. He was, after all, in no rush. He had all the time in the world. And while he planned to kill Dana Polson, he could do it later—next week, next month.

Well, it wouldn't be next month. He was pretty sure of that.

He was pretty sure he'd be completely blind by then. He felt it getting worse and worse. It had for years now…and that's why he had finally decided to go about this business. He had to take care of it before he went blind.

Depending on how today's reading went…that's how he'd know when he would strike. Building up trust was important. He couldn't just act without thought or forming some sort of relationship. He'd learned that the hard way with Cleo Colegrove. Simply studying her routine and schedule had not been enough. He'd started studying her routines after she had passed him while he had been visiting Servant's Heart Ministries to see what they were all about. The way she had looked at him…he'd felt it. She'd known about the things he had done. Her sightless eyes had lingered on him a little too long for his comfort.

He'd hoped he would be successful with Cleo, proving that he didn't have to waste the time in getting to know his victims before he struck. That way, he could dispatch more of them before he lost his sight completely.

But he had been wrong. So even if it was just one or two reading sessions, he had to take the time to build up a level of friendship and trust with his victims. Ellis Ridgeway was the perfect example. He'd been reading to her for two months before he finally struck—and she had never seen it coming. Even at the end, when she took her last breath and her sightless eyes had searched for meaning behind what was happening to her, she had not known.

Soon enough, he'd see that same blank yet terrified look in the eyes of Dana Polson.

He thought of what it might look like even as he read to her.

And he couldn't help but wonder if it's what his own eyes might look like on the day he took his final breaths.

CHAPTER TWENTY ONE

This is ridiculous, Mackenzie thought as she and Ellington walked back into the Wakeman Home for the Blind. There was an air of tension between them now and it reminded her of the high school drama of careless teenage romances. Sure, her heart hurt at the thought of the way she had spoken to him in the car on the way here but at the same time, she also realized that it was foolish.

That's how she was so easily able to push past it and focus on the case—on the quiet and saddened halls of Wakeman. In a morose sort of way, she was almost glad to be back in a quiet place like this, even if that quiet *was* the result of sadness brought on by a death.

Before they could even make it to the small receptionist's desk, Randall Jones came walking down the hallway. There was an older woman with him, walking slightly behind him with a hunch to her back. She walked with a cane that made little musical thumps as she progressed down the hallway. Randall looked over his shoulder to make sure she was doing okay and then greeted Mackenzie and Ellington at the desk.

"Hi, Agents," he said. "Sheriff Clarke told me that you might want to speak with this young lady." He then turned to the old woman behind him and gave a prideful smile. "Agents White and Ellington, meet Nina Brady."

"It's good to meet you," Mackenzie said. "Do you mind speaking with us about a few things?"

"Is it about Ellis?" Nina asked. Her voice was sweet but ragged, showing her age and suggesting years of heavy smoking.

"It is," Mackenzie said.

"Then yes, I'd love to speak with you. Of course, I'd prefer if Randall stayed with me. I hope you understand that for a blind person, it's hard as hell to trust anyone after hearing that a blind friend of yours was killed out of what appears to be plain old meanness."

"That's perfectly understandable," Ellington said.

Nina smiled, turning her head in Ellington's direction. "Mmm-hmm. Randall, this boy sounds handsome. Good build?"

"Ms. Brady, let's not do that."

Nina chuckled and shook her head. "Mr. Agent, would you mind escorting an old lady to the sofa in the common room?" She extended her arm, as if waiting for a suitor to link his own arm through it.

"Yes ma'am," Ellington obliged, taking her gently by the arm as if stepping out on the town with a date. Mackenzie couldn't help but smile.

Randall led the way to the common room that sat on the back of the building. A large picture window looked out onto a small flower garden and a large expanse of grass and thick forests beyond. Ellington assisted Nina to her seat while Mackenzie and Randall took their own seats in small recliners across from the couch. There was only one other person in the community room, a resident who was listening to something on an iPad with earbuds in while staring out toward the flower garden.

She noticed that Ellington opted to sit next to Nina and did not even look in her direction. He was being intentionally cold and as far as Mackenzie was concerned in that moment, she honestly didn't care. Mackenzie looked beyond this, refusing to be pulled into any sort of needless drama.

"Ms. Brady, I'll be honest with you here. Ellis was not the only blind person to have been murdered lately. There have been three murders over the course of two weeks. And just yesterday, a woman in Lynchburg was attacked by a man we believe to be the killer."

"Oh my God," Nina said, on the verge of tears.

"This killer is either very smart or very lucky," Mackenzie went on. "We have no evidence, no leads, and no real idea of where to even look next. We heard that you were friends with Mrs. Ridgeway, so I was hoping you might be able to offer some insights that we might have overlooked. If there is anything at all you can think of about her—of things she did or said in her last few days that seemed peculiar—that would be a huge help."

"Well, Ellis was a peculiar lady anyway," Nina said. "But in the absolute best way."

"How so?" Mackenzie asked.

"Well, she often acted a little immature. She made jokes that a teenage kids might make. She loved those Harry Potter books and was very into the whole thing...being sorted into houses and quoting the books around here."

"Did she read a lot?" Mackenzie asked, realizing how utterly stupid the question sounded the moment it was out of her mouth.

Nina picked up on this and chuckled. "Well, she listened to lots of audiobooks. But she much preferred to have other people read to her."

"Who read to her? Caretakers here?"

"Sometimes. I believe last summer she had a high school girl come by and read to her. She *really* enjoyed that. And then not too

110

long ago, there was someone else that came by and started reading to her. A young man, I think."

"How long ago?" Mackenzie asked.

"Quite recently. I'd even go so far as to say that he was here a day, maybe two, before she died."

For the first time since coming back into Wakeman, Mackenzie and Ellington looked at one another. Mackenzie then looked to Randall Jones and asked: "Do you know who it was?"

"Not right offhand. We have a name in our records, though. In the visitor log."

"Oh, his name was Robbie, I believe," Nina said. "Ellis liked him quite a bit. He was a volunteer with an organization called—"

"Servant's Heart," Mackenzie said.

"That's exactly right," Nina said.

She looked delighted that she had helped make the connection, but the look on Mackenzie's face was the total opposite. It came back to Robbie Huston, whom she had already ruled out. Another dead end.

However, the concept of the visitors' log intrigued her. Even if they didn't know what name to look for specifically, maybe there would be something there that they didn't even know to look for.

She got to her feet, her eyes still on Randall Jones.

"Let's go take a look at your visitors' log," she said.

***

Mackenzie had only ever seen Randall Jones as helpful, empathetic, and encouraging of his residents. So to see him livid and seething ten minutes later was rather jarring. He held the visitors' log in his hand—the actual physical book—while scrolling maniacally through the digital sign-ins as well.

He was fuming over the check-in counter as one of the caretakers—a young woman who currently looked terrified—stood wide-eyed and paralyzed.

"We have one resident confirming the visit of a volunteer one or two days before Ellis Ridgeway was killed," he said. "So tell me how in the name of God there is no name in the visitors' log?"

"I don't know," the young girl said. "Which volunteer are you—"

"The one who came to read to Ellis!"

"Oh, yes, I remember him coming in. He was the short guy, the really quiet man with the cane."

"Cane?" Mackenzie asked. She wanted to make sure she had heard them correctly because if so, that was a huge help in their search for the killer.

"Yes, I think so."

"The volunteer I had in mind was a young man. Maybe mid-twenties."

"No, that's Robbie," the young girl said. "This is a totally different man. Older...maybe in his mid-thirties. No older than forty. And he does walk with a cane."

"Shit," Randall said, slamming the visitors' log down on the counter.

"You know who she's talking about?" Mackenzie asked.

"Yeah. And it's for sure not Robbie Huston. This guy's name is Ian Osborne. He's pretty nice, too. I've never really spoken at length with him. All I know is that he says he used to have issues with his vision because of a tumor. He stands at around five-eight or so, I'd guess. I always assumed that the troubles he had with the tumor and his vision made him sort of sympathetic to the residents. But look...I've spoken with him. There's no way it was him. He's too damned kind."

"Well, that may be the case," Mackenzie said. "But we have a man that your employees are saying was here very close to Mrs. Ridgeway's death and you have no actual records of it. That makes him a suspect."

"Let me check something really quickly," Randall said. He flipped through the guest log, scanning each page as he went. His finger tore down the pages and he got more and more frustrated with every page he turned. Finally, he stopped and threw his hands up in the air, as if giving up.

"I feel like I need to apologize," he said. "Ian's name is only on here once—and that's from four months ago. And even though I know for a fact he's been here at least half a dozen times, that's the last time his name is actually in the records."

He looked up at the receptionist with a scathing heat in his eyes.

"Well, I can't speak for everyone that sits behind this desk," the woman said, "but it's like you said. He was a nice man...put you at ease, you know? Really friendly. I guess we just never checked the logs after he came to make sure he had signed it."

Randall rubbed at his temples, like he was staving off a headache. He then looked to Mackenzie and Ellington with a frown, the anger now melting away. "I'm sorry," he said. "We have no records of him coming in here for the past four months, although I can conform he's been here at least six times. Maybe more."

It was a bit disappointing not to have the dates that this new man—Ian Osborne—had visited, but that was okay. She now had a name and a very astute medical history to go on. Tracking down a man who volunteered his time to the blind *and* had a medical history that included a tumor would be very easy to track down.

"Mr. Jones?" the woman asked.

"Yes?" he asked, clearly annoyed.

"You know, there was that one other man. The one with the glass eye..."

"That's right," Randall said. "He was newer, though...right?"

"Right," the woman said.

"Do you recall his name?"

She shook her head. "I'm pretty sure it was something like Ken or Carl. Maybe Keith? He was pretty quiet. I never really spoke to him." She hesitated. "It, um, looks like his name isn't in the log either."

"What about the other caretakers or receptionists?" Mackenzie asked. "Did they ever speak with him?"

"I don't know," she said.

"Jesus, don't we just look like we run a tight ship around here?" Randall said, getting up from the chair behind the desk with such force that it sent the chair skidding back against the wall.

"This other man," Mackenzie said, doing her best to look past the absolute negligence of Wakeman's record keeping. "You said he has a glass eye?"

"Yes," the woman said.

"And when was the last time you saw him?"

"Oh, I'm not sure. A few days, maybe?"

"How about you, Mr. Jones?" Ellington asked.

"If he was a volunteer, I only step in during the paperwork part. Once they're approved, I ask the residents what they think of them—sort of a feedback session. So long as they're happy, I'm happy."

"Okay," Mackenzie said, now more frustrated than ever. "I need to speak with every resident here," she said. "And then I need to see the paperwork on every volunteer that has come in here to read to the residents—whether individually or through an organization like Servant's Heart. And at the risk of seeming like a bitch, I need it all done *now*."

Randall nodded and got to his feet. "I'll get everyone in the common room. Maybe it'll go faster with everyone in one place."

Mackenzie nodded, turning to look at Ellington. "Anything else?" she asked.

He was holding his phone and frowning. He nodded and said, "Yeah. We just got a text from McGrath...and he's pissed."

CHAPTER TWENTY TWO

First an angry backwoods politician, then Ellington, and now McGrath, Mackenzie thought as she dialed up McGrath's number. *I wonder who else I can manage to piss off today.*

As the phone started ringing in her ear, she stepped out of the Wakeman Home for the Blind and into the blazing Virginia sun. Ellington was behind her and in order to save any frustration or confusion, she placed the call on speakerphone.

McGrath answered on the fourth ring and wasted no time with formalities.

"Does the name Langston Ridgeway ring any bells for you, White?"

"Yes, sir," she said, not bothering with trying to make things seem prettier than they were. "I spoke with him about half an hour ago. A real piece of shit. Thinks he's a lot more of a man than he actually is."

"I don't care what you think of him," he said. "You're down there to investigate his mother's death and you threw a business card at him?"

"In all fairness," Ellington said, "I threw the business card at him."

"That's unacceptable," McGrath said. "And furthermore, another thing that is unacceptable is that you've been on this thing for nearly four days now and all you have to show for it is an endless stream of driving. Need I remind you that this is a case and not some getaway chance for romance?"

"That's absolutely right, sir. But this killer is moving all over the place."

"But you're back in Stateton now?" he asked.

"Yes, sir. The case led us back here to speak with one of the other residents."

"And did it produce anything?"

"We don't know yet, sir."

There was a silence on the line for a moment before McGrath responded again. "Four days with no results is too much for my liking, especially when you're antagonizing the loved ones of the recently deceased. I'm giving you another twenty-four hours before I pull you back in and send someone else down to do your jobs. You're both too talented to be stuck down in this raging hell right now."

"Sir, if you'll—" Mackenzie began.

"One day," he interrupted.

"No problem," Ellington said, turning on his heel and heading for the car.

"White?" McGrath said.

"Yes, sir."

With that, McGrath ended the call. Mackenzie stared at the phone in frustration and then to Ellington.

"Where the hell are you going?" she asked.

"To pack up," he said. "You're more than welcome to stay down here in this muggy heat and run around in circles."

"You can't be serious right now."

He sighed and came back toward her, standing in front of the doors into the Wakeman. "I don't know any way to say this without coming off as overdramatic, but given the current state of our relationship, it seems dumb for me to stick around. I'll just get in the way."

"You mean just because I'm not ready to move in with you?"

"Among other things."

"What other things?" she asked. "Jesus, Ellington…this is ridiculous."

"Yeah, it is," he said. "And I'm sorry for that. Look…I'm just trying to be honest with you here."

"And you can just leave? Just like that?"

"Might as well," he said. "You heard McGrath. Twenty-four hours and we're off of this. And given the way things have gone on this case so far, twenty-four hours isn't nearly enough. So I figure I'll save myself some grief and leave now."

"I'm staying," she said matter-of-factly.

"I figured you would. I'll take this car to the station and have Clarke come pick you up. I'll get a rental from somewhere."

She barely heard these final logistics. She was far too flooded with emotions: anger, frustration, sorrow, confusion. She felt like screaming but was too confused to do so. Even her lungs seemed to be momentarily frozen by the abruptness of the moment.

Is this my fault? Am I pushing him away?

It was a question that snuck up on her, taking her by surprise. Worse than that, though, was the fact that even if it *was* the case, she didn't really care. Maybe she wasn't ready for a relationship just yet. Maybe she would be one of those women who was essentially married to her job.

She nearly called out to him, asking him to stay. But she could not bring herself to do it. Besides…it was pretty clear that he didn't want to be here in that moment.

In the end, she said nothing. She turned her back on him and walked inside. Yes, it hurt to leave him behind, knowing this could very well end their relationship. But she would not allow herself to be consumed by it. There was a killer out there and she felt like he was a ghost—a force that had managed to completely elude her so far. And the one thing that had not changed about Mackenzie since getting involved with Ellington was that work came first.

Work would always come first.

She took a moment to collect herself before she walked into the common room. She found the ladies' room in the small waiting area out front and hurried into it. She locked the door behind her and simply stared at herself in the mirror. As she did so, she found herself thinking about a cornfield back in Nebraska, the place where her longer story had more or less began. That was where she had seen that first body, the first victim of the Scarecrow Killer. That had been a little more than two years ago, yet it seemed like another lifetime.

I thought we'd never catch that bastard, she thought. And with that thought, she could almost feel the silk-like surface of the cornstalks and smell the churned earth beneath her feet.

She took a deep breath, focusing herself and getting her thoughts in order. *I thought we'd never catch him, but we did. I did. And I'll catch this one, too.*

She forged on and entered the common room, where Randall Jones and two caretakers were aiding the residents to their seats. Oddly enough, without Ellington with her, she felt more alone than she had suspected.

And maybe that was a good thing.

CHAPTER TWENTY THREE

With nothing more of value discovered at Wakeman, Mackenzie stepped back out into the rugged heat. She saw Sheriff Clarke parked in the exact same spot Ellington's car had been parked in half an hour earlier. Clarke was sitting behind the wheel, his head craned back comfortably. The engine was running and she could hear the air conditioning plugging away. As she approached the passenger side door and opened it, she saw that he had not been napping. He was simply staring at the cruiser's roof, deep in thought.

"I take it you're my ride back to the station?" Mackenzie asked him.

"Seems that way. Ellington left the car for you. A cab picked him up ten minutes ago. I've been out here waiting for you ever since."

She got into the car, enjoying the feel of the police cruiser. She'd started her career out in one of these and everything from the stale smell from the back to the hiss and crackle of the dashboard CB system was warmly comforting.

"Sorry about whatever beef is going on between you two," Clarke said. He sounded as if he sincerely meant it. "Anyway...where to now?"

"Back to the PD for now, I think. Randall and his people are going through their files for a bit of information for me. It shouldn't take too long. In the meantime, I'll call one of my guys back at Quantico and have him try to expedite things to help them. And if I could bum a desk off of you, I'll just go over the files until something—"

She stopped when she heard her name, muffled through the blast of the cruiser's air conditioning and the windshield. She looked across the small yard in front of the home and saw Randall Jones running toward them. He was waving a sheet of paper at her like some deranged newsboy from the 1920s.

Mackenzie rolled the window down as he came to the car. Randall held the sheet out to her, rather proud of himself. "We apparently need to crack down on our visitor sign-in policies," he said, "but we *do* keep a tidy records database. The volunteer with the glass eye is named Carl Windham. I have no address and the phone number on record is dead—we already tried it—but we *do* have the name of the agency that sent him."

"That'll do for now," she said. "Thanks, Mr. Jones."

"Of course. I just wish we could have helped more...and sooner."

She didn't tell him that this might be the most reliable lead they'd had the entire time. But as she looked at the information, it clearly was. "Thanks, Mr. Jones," she said again, and rolled up the window.

"That a solid lead?" Clarke asked as he reversed the car out of the lot.

"It might just be," she said.

She looked to the address and sighed.

Bedford, she thought. If her mind was recalling the Virginia map correctly, Bedford was a small town about twenty miles outside of Lynchburg. Wherever it was, it likely meant that she'd be driving again before the day was through.

For now, though, she'd hopefully be able to maintain the case via a phone call from the Stateton police station.

***

The station was a small place, so there was no loaner office. Instead, Clarke seemed happy to offer his own office. When Mackenzie tried to refuse it, he gave her a scowling sort of frown and shook his head.

"I seriously don't mind," he insisted. "I'd much rather be out front, drinking coffee with Frances and catching up on the town gossip. Just please be sure to let me know if you need anything."

With that, Clarke had taken up a position up front while Mackenzie sat in his well-worn chair behind a desk that looked like it might be older than she was. The first thing she did was call the number of the agency on the sheet Randall Jones had given her. It was the number for a place called The Guiding Sight Agency and Temp Service. While the phone started to ring, she pulled out her state map of Virginia, folded intricately in the file folder she had kept all of the notes in to this point. With each piece unfolded, more and more of Clarke's desk was swallowed up. By the time she had most of it revealed, the phone was answered on the other end.

"Guiding Sight," said a tired-sounding woman. "How can I help you?"

"Hello. This is Agent Mackenzie White with the FBI. I'm currently working on a case that has brought one of your volunteers to my attention. Who do I need to speak to about this?"

"That would be me," the woman said. "Kate Briggs. I run the ship around here. We're not a very big agency. Who is the volunteer you're looking for?"

"A man named Carl Windham. As I understand it, he has a glass eye."

There was silence on the end of the line for a moment, a suspicious quiet that told Mackenzie she was definitely on to something.

"Ms. Briggs?"

"I'm here. Yes. Carl used to be a volunteer for us."

"Used to? As in not anymore?"

"That's right."

"Might I ask why he is no longer with the agency?"

"I'm sorry," Briggs said. "I need to know that I am indeed speaking with an agent before I reveal that kind of information. Could you perhaps meet in person?"

"Ms. Briggs, I have been all over the state of Virginia for the last three days. I am currently stationed in Stateton, about two hours away from you. I'd really rather not waste more of my time on the road and, more than that, would like to not allow a murderer that extra amount of time to get further away or, worse than that, strike again."

"I understand that, but I—"

"No, I don't think you do," Mackenzie said. "Look…I'm Agent Mackenzie White. My section chief is a man named McGrath. My badge number is two-three-seven—"

"Excuse me," Briggs said. "But if you are really an FBI agent, you know that giving out personal information over the phone about people that have signed on to be part of my organization can be considered unlawful. I am not risking myself or my company by offering that sort of information. So unless I can *see* a badge and an actual person face-to-face, you're not getting anything from me."

Mackenzie bit down the rage that tried to push forward. Through clenched teeth, she said: "When I arrive there in two hours, I want you to remember how difficult you were. If I were a real bitch, I could have you arrested for interfering in a government investigation."

Briggs started to say something else, but Mackenzie hung up. She tossed her phone down onto Clarke's desk and muttered an angry slur of curse words under her breath.

She looked down to the map, grabbed a pen from a coffee mug on Clarke's desk, and circled each area of attack. *Stateton. Treston. Richmond. Lynchburg.* As far as she could tell, there was no real pattern. The inclusion of Lynchburg in the list ruled out the factor that all the cities contained homes for the blind.

There was nothing of substance to be found on the map.

What the hell am I missing?

She stared at the map for another two minutes, trying to think like a killer. Maybe the locations all had some ties to the killer. Or maybe he knew them all somehow—an improbable theory, given that they were all blind people. And really...how many average, perfectly healthy people knew a blind person?

Then it has *to be the fact that they are blind. It's not the people and their identities. It never has been. It's* because *they are blind. He's killing them because they are blind.*

"But why?" she wondered.

Maybe he thinks he's doing them a favor. Maybe he sees them as mercy killings. Or maybe it scares him for some reason. That seems like more of a stretch but definitely a possibility.

The map had offered up nothing. She might as well be staring at a brick wall. She folded it back up, tucked all of her notes inside of it, and headed for the front of the building. As much as she hated it, she had yet another road trip to take.

CHAPTER TWENTY FOUR

Mackenzie stewed in her anger for the entire hour and forty-five minutes it took her to reach Bedford. Getting there, she bypassed Lynchburg, making her feel as if she was trapped in some weird loop, reminding her of Bill Murray in *Groundhog Day*. She could feel the twenty-four hours McGrath had given her slipping away with each mile and did everything within her power to remain calm and forward-thinking.

She arrived in Bedford around noon. It was a quaint little town, the sort that was steeped in history but also seemed to be a bit progressive in some of its businesses. She located Guiding Sight on the far corner of a cute but seemingly forgotten street that was punctuated with antique stores and an insurance agent's office.

She was half expecting Kate Briggs to not be there. Maybe the idea of an angry FBI agent headed her way would cause her to close up shop for the day. However, the door was unlocked, leading directly into a small waiting area. The air conditioner was blasting, which was a blessing considering that it was easily ninety-five in the shade outside.

A woman sat behind a small desk, typing something into a laptop. She looked up, saw Mackenzie, and got to her feet instantly. She was a tall middle-aged lady with a head full of strawberry blonde hair. The thin-rimmed glasses she wore made her look a bit like a librarian.

"Kate Briggs?" Mackenzie asked.

"Yes. And you're Agent Wh—"

Mackenzie took out her badge and practically shoved it in Kate's face. Kate took a step back and then let out a shaky sigh. "Well, you don't have to be so menacing about it!"

"Forgive me," Mackenzie said. "But you just wasted two hours of my time on a day where I am on a tight deadline to try to stop a killer before he kills someone else. A killer that, by the way, seems to be targeting only blind people."

"I can appreciate your situation, but I also have to protect the privacy of the people that volunteer for me."

"I'm sure," Mackenzie said. "But what I found very interesting was the extremely long pause that fell over the phone when I told you who I was calling to ask about."

Kate reeled a bit, steadying herself against her desk. It was clear that she wasn't used to being pushed around this way.

"Carl Windham," Mackenzie said. "Who is he?"

Kate stepped behind her desk and offered Mackenzie several sheets of paper. The piece on top appeared to be an application of some kind. It had been filled out on May 20, 2014, by Carl Windham. According to the information he had filled in, he'd been twenty-six years old when he applied.

"Carl was someone that I believed to be very passionate about those in need," Kate said. "And I may as well divulge this, because I'm sure it would come up sooner or later—he and I had a relationship for about three months."

"Define *relationship*," Mackenzie said.

"Strictly sexual," Kate answered, blushing a bit. "No dating, just fairly frequent sex."

Maybe she has no problem admitting it because she's easily forty-five and she was having sex with someone at least twelve years younger than her.

"Did the relationship occur before or after he applied to volunteer?"

"After," she said. "He'd been here for about a month and a half before anything happened between us."

"Is the relationship why he left?"

"No," Kate said. "I asked him to leave when one of our clients complained that he was threatening her. She said he was a little crude in the way he talked to her and would sometimes curse at her."

"And you believed her at face value?"

"Not right away. But then another woman called and said he's tried taking advantage of her."

"And both of these clients were blind?"

"Yes."

"Is that the only group you cater to here?"

"Yes. We do it in several ways. I have a pool of volunteers that do just about anything for people in the blind community within about one hundred miles or so. We have some people that mow lawns for the blind, go grocery shopping for them, serve as temporary caretakers...that sort of thing."

"What about Carl? What kinds of things did he do?"

"A bit of everything," Kate said. "He started off by mowing lawns and somehow ended up reading to a few clients. They really seemed to enjoy it."

"And what sort of qualifications do your volunteers need to have in order to be a part of Guiding Sight?"

"It depends on what they plan to do," she said. "For Carl, like I said, he started out by just mowing lawns. So I asked for some references, which he provided. I also had a background check done, as I do with all of my applicants, and that checked out."

Mackenzie scanned the application. She paid close attention the *Previous Work History* section. Carl Windham had cut the grass for his local church, keeping the cemetery maintained. He also had some experience in small engine repair. When he was twenty-two, he worked as an assistant groundskeeper for a high school in a rural community.

"How long ago did you release him as a volunteer?" Mackenzie asked.

"It's been about eight months or so, I'd guess."

"And one of the details I have about him is he had a glass eye. Is that correct?"

"Yes, though he sometimes wore an eye patch instead."

"Do you know how he lost the eye?"

"Some sort of freak accident while mowing the grass for a church where he grew up. From what he told me, a piece of rock broke off under the blade and ricocheted off of the undercarriage. It came flying out and popped him right in the eye. That's his story anyway...though I never really believed him."

"Why not?"

Kate shrugged. "I don't know, really. I just...I could tell he was lying. He never really wanted to talk about it."

"When you heard the reports from your clients about his misconduct, did it come as a surprise? Does he have the kind of personality that sort of indicated there might be something about him that was a little off?"

"Here and there, I suppose. He had a passion for the blind because he lost his sight for a while when he was a child. He never said as much, but I think when he lost his eye, he felt like it was a sign...from God or the universe or whatever. He got sort of weird and deep like that sometimes. Also, there were things he...well, things he wanted to do in the bedroom that I declined. Things that took me by surprise."

There's nothing sexual to these attacks, though, Mackenzie thought. *Although, if he was cut loose or rejected by a lover because of deplorable behavior, a leaning toward sexual deviancy could easily become violent and aggressive.*

"Do you have an address for him?" she asked.

A slight touch of regret touched Kate's face as she nodded. "I do. I know exactly where he lives. No one would hire him after the mess with the blind women, so he works from home. Engine and mower repair out of his garage, in addition to the government assistance for the accident with his eye. And it turns out you didn't waste a trip to Bedford. We're currently about ten minutes from his house."

CHAPTER TWENTY FIVE

Mackenzie parked her car on the side of the street in front of a single-story white house. It was well maintained and had an immaculate yard, proof of Windham's history of taking care of lawns. A single pickup truck sat in his small concrete driveway, black splotches showing the ghosts of past oil changes.

She got out of her car and walked up to the cracked concrete steps. The stairs, like the rest of the house, were clearly old but well cared for. The porch gave slightly beneath her as he approached the door and knocked.

"Yeah!" came a voice from inside. It was a male and it sounded fairly cheerful. "One second!"

Mackenzie listened to someone approaching from the other side of the door and when it was answered, it was not the sort of man she had been expecting. Carl Windham was obviously under thirty years of age and was quite handsome, even with the eye patch. He looked at Mackenzie, puzzled.

"Hello? How can I help you?"

Mackenzie flashed her badge. "I'm Agent White with the FBI," she said, finding it odd to have to cut herself off before introducing the absent Agent Ellington. "I'm looking into a case and your name happened to come up."

He frowned; it was an expression she had seen at least one hundred times before. It was the frown of a man who thought he had lived long enough to creep out from under the shadows of his past only to have the past sneak back up on his heels and swallow him whole.

"Yes, I know about the accusations in your past," she said.

"More than accusations," he said. "They're all true. I did it. I'm obviously not proud of it, but I did it."

"Well, regardless, that's not precisely why I'm here. I'm here because your name came up as a past volunteer with Guiding Sight. And recently, there was a murder at a home for the blind where your name was listed on the guest register."

She left out the part about his name not being there for a couple of months. Hopefully he'd stumble and offer up valuable details.

"Oh my God. Was it Wakeman?"

"It was," Mackenzie said. "How did you know?"

"Well, that was the last home I volunteered at."

She noticed that he was tensing up. Also, he had not yet invited her into his house. She looked for any signs of distress or fear on his

126

face but saw none. She felt almost like she was being discriminatory when she realized that the lack of a right eye made it very hard to judge his expression accurately.

"Mr. Windham, can I please come inside?"

He appeared to think about this for a moment and then looked outside, up and down the street, in a quick motion. *He's ashamed of his past,* she thought. *He doesn't want anyone seeing a woman dressed liked this—clearly a government official—walking into his house.*

"Yeah, I guess that would be okay."

He led her inside the small house but he was not the happy-looking man who had answered the door. He now looked fidgety and preoccupied. He brought her into the kitchen area and opened the fridge. She took a seat at the table, hoping that seeing her in a relaxed position might help him to relax.

Windham took a can of soda out of the fridge, plucked it open, and took a chug from it.

"Mr. Windham, when was the last time you visited the Wakeman Home for the Blind?"

He seemed to put genuine thought into his answer as he swallowed down his massive gulp of soda. "Maybe eight or nine months?"

Lines up with what Kate Briggs told me, Mackenzie thought. *But not what Randall Jones and the residents at Wakeman have told me.*

"I'll give you a moment to take that back and tell me the truth," Mackenzie said. "I've spoken with the management and the residents at Wakeman. And they say that they have seen one of the reading volunteers quite recently. There have been two there fairly regularly over the past couple of months. One of them was described as a younger man with a glass eye. And you, Mr. Windham, are the only person to volunteer there that has a glass eye. So I ask you again: when was the last time you visited Wakeman?"

He took another drink from the soda, just a basic stalling tactic. As he raised the can to his mouth, she saw his arm trembling.

When he brought it away, she saw that he was weeping. "I didn't do anything wrong. Not after I was arrested for the other stuff I did. I've been clean of it. I went back to Wakeman because the women there at the desk liked me. I knew I could get around signing a guest book. I just missed reading to them. There was one woman there in particular that really enjoyed it when I read to her. Mrs. Ridgeway. She was…"

He trailed off here. It was a good thing too, because Mackenzie was on high alert. *He just confessed to having read to Ellis Ridgeway. This could be it. This could be the guy.*

She wanted to believe that but something about him didn't add up.

"Ellis Ridgeway was the woman who was murdered from Wakeman," she said.

His reaction told her everything she needed to know. Carl Windham was many things...but he was not the killer. He looked genuinely heartbroken and a little confused. He also looked pissed that she had decided to tell him in such a way.

"When?" he said.

"Five days ago. And I've been looking for the killer ever since."

"It wasn't me," he said. "I loved that dear old lady. I...she's dead? Who would do such a thing?"

High standards from a man who sexually assaulted two blind women, she thought.

"I don't know," she said. "But I'd like for you to answer my original question and answer it honestly. When was the last time you went to Wakeman?"

"A little over a week ago."

"You're absolutely sure of that?"

He nodded, but absently. He looked zoned out, staring at the soda can in his hand. "I knew I shouldn't," he said. "I never told them that I was no longer with Guiding Sight and they never asked. They just assumed everything was fine and okay. Everything in the courts with the others was settled. I got arrested, paid a fine and penalties. Did a tiny little stint in jail. But it wasn't big news. The people at Wakeman never knew. And I guess Kate...well, she never broadcast it, either. Why would she? That would look terrible for Guiding Sight, now wouldn't it?"

"You're right," Mackenzie said, getting to her feet. "It *was* wrong. And given everything that's happened—"

"That's not who I am anymore! I'm done! I'm clean of it and that's *NOT ME!*"

He screamed it, the words as sudden as a bomb. It startled Mackenzie and had her reaching for her sidearm. At the same time, in a nearly comedic moment, Windham threw the can of soda at her. It struck her in the head and, because it was half-empty at that point, only pissed her off, stupefied her for about two seconds, and got the side of her face wet and sticky with cola.

"Mr. Windham," she said, "you're making this so much worse than it has to be. Just stop right there and—"

"It's not me! I'm not like that anymore!"

And before she knew it, he was rushing at her. He did it with such speed and surprise that she barely had time to even reach for her gun. He tried punching her in the face, but she blocked it. He then slapped her hard in the side of the face and tried throwing a knee up, which she also blocked.

While blocking his knee, she grabbed his leg, cupped her hands under it, and leaned down. She then pulled up on his leg and sent him sprawling to the floor. As he went, he flailed for the table. Mackenzie realized a bit too late that it wasn't to grasp for balance. He had grabbed a decorative bowl.

She realized this only after it smashed into the side of her head. It was heavy and thick and sent black trails of stars rocketing across her vision. She scrambled to keep purchase of him but he was off of her in a flash. She went for her Glock, blinking away those black stars, but Windham was already out of the back door by the fridge.

Well, that escalated quickly, she thought in a dizzy sort of confusion.

She got to her feet, her head still reeling. She took a moment to steady herself against the refrigerator and then followed him outside. She drew her Glock as she walked out onto a tiny back porch. She saw a small shed at the far end of his yard, the doors slamming shut. She went down the porch steps and into the yard as her head finally started to clear up. The heat pressed down on her, radiating so intensely that she thought she could feel the waves of it as the sun blazed its angry eye at this side of the world.

Ellington would have gotten a kick out of this, she thought, wiping soda away from her face. She could smell its sweetness in the heat soaked into the collar of her shirt.

She stopped before she reached the shed. She couldn't react on her anger and embarrassment alone. Without Ellington, she had to take a different approach here. Going in alone could cause more problems. Who knew what a man that unbalanced might have in his shed?

Still…she was pissed. And when she got good and angry, she was rarely able to contain it. A stream of curse words buzzed in her head like hornets as her knuckles tightened around the Glock.

"Damn," she muttered, pulling out her phone while keeping her eyes glued to the shed.

Before she had time to come up with a plan of attack, she heard something that was the last thing she'd expected: an engine, revving from inside the shed.

"Hold it right there!" she screamed, training her gun at the shed doors.

One of the doors popped open as the engine noise increased.

What is that? A motorcycle?

She got her answer two seconds later as Windham came barreling out of the shed on an old Harley. The bike was in bad shape and as Windham directed out of the shed with speed, it wobbled. But the fucking thing was coming right at her. The scene was so surreal that Mackenzie was slow to react.

No other choice, she thought.

She fired off a shot as Windham guided the bike directly toward her.

She heard a *clang* over the roar of the engine as her shot hit the bike and ricocheted elsewhere. Then the bike was past her, headed for the road.

He wasn't trying to run me down, she thought. *The bastard is trying to escape.*

Luckily, he wasn't going quite as fast as he wanted, as the bike was still wobbling a bit as he tried getting around the house in a panic.

Mackenzie took off after him, seeing a window of opportunity that didn't end with her having to explain a dead civilian to McGrath.

She sprinted as quickly as her stunned legs would allow, her head once again deciding that it was in pain from the blow from the bowl. When she was close enough to the bike to worry that the back tire would strike her knee, she lunged out and to the left.

Her feet left the ground and both hands landed on Windham's shoulders. They both went to the ground in a heap, but her hands never left Windham's shoulders. She struck her side, sending the air out of her, but she still pushed him hard into the ground. With his back to her, she delivered a hard knee into his ribs and then pulled his arms behind his back.

Her heart was slamming in her chest and she could literally taste the adrenaline, salty and like a chemical in her throat. Despite this, her muscles were calm and steady as she slapped her handcuffs around his wrists

Keeping her gun trained on him and not yet speaking directly to him, she pulled her phone out and gave a voice command to call the Bedford Police Department.

She heard Windham whimpering from the ground. He'd gone limp and was starting to break...his whimpers becoming choked sobs.

Her gun remained aimed on him as her phone started to ring in her ear.

***

Mackenzie was calm and collected by the time the two patrol cars came screeching to a stop in front of Carl Windham's house. Her head ached and her left side was sore, but it had been worth it. She was pretty damned sure she had her man, still sobbing at her feet with his hands cuffed behind his back.

After a brief line of questions from the three officers that showed up, Mackenzie walked up onto the back porch, wanting to look around inside the house. Honestly, the whole thing felt anticlimactic...even after she had been nearly run down by an aged Harley Davidson (which had coasted into the street and struck the neighbor's mailbox before clattering to the pavement).

As she watched the cops haul Windham up to his feet and out of the yard, Mackenzie found herself wishing that Ellington was there. Everything within her told her that Windham lined up—he fit what they were looking for and, after all, he had reacted in a way that was guilty, though not in the textbook way she had been looking for. Still...she couldn't help but feel that it had been too easy...like it had practically fallen into her lap. There was something about Windham that didn't quite jive with the three murders and the attack on Cleo Colegrove.

It made her think he had something to hide—if not several murders, then certainly *something*. It would be nice to share the victory with Ellington.

"So we'll haul his ass down to the PD," one of the cops said as they walked around the side of the house. "There'll be some paperwork for you. And of course, you get first swing at questioning him."

Mackenzie nodded. "I appreciate it. I'll be a few minutes behind you. I want to check out his house to see if there's anything worth finding."

"Sure," the cop said. "And hey...awesome job."

"Thanks," she said absently as she headed back up the porch stairs and into the house.

She entered through the kitchen, eyeing the soda can that he had thrown at her. The remainder of its contents had spilled out onto the linoleum floor. She stepped past this and walked down a thin hallway. She skipped the living room, assuming that anything incriminating would not be in the house's central room.

Along the hallway, she found a bathroom, a bedroom, and a smaller bedroom that served as a small office of sorts. She entered the office and found a laptop, opened and powered up on the desk. When she clicked the mouse to make the sleep screen vanish, she couldn't believe her luck. Not only did the laptop not require a password to resume the previous sessions after it had gone to sleep, but Windham had apparently been checking his email when she had come knocking.

She looked through the mails in his Gmail account, looking through the inbox as well as his sent mails. She then found a categories label for Guiding Sight. Most of them were harmless emails, detailing visits he would be making to Wakeman and the Mary Denbridge Home. They were all from several months ago and there was no email evidence that he had visited anytime recently.

She also found a few emails from Kate Briggs, dated several months ago as well. Some of them were promiscuous in nature, hinting at future dates they were going to meet as well as referring to previous trysts. One of the emails contained an attachment of a picture of Kate Briggs in bed, in a compromising position and wearing hardly anything.

She clicked away from the picture quickly and then pulled up the laptop's file directory. Windham kept a tidy laptop, everything tucked away in its own folders. A quick search showed nothing incriminating. She then looked in the desk drawers and found them just as tidy. That was how she was able to find the memory stick so quickly. It was the only one in sight, making it that much more interesting.

She plugged it into the laptop, opened the disc contents, and found a series of documents not filed away in folders. When she saw that the documents were movie files, she was pretty sure she might be on to something.

Let's just hope it's not more lurid content featuring Kate Briggs, she thought.

There were eleven files. She opened only one before she realized what she had stumbled upon. Thirty seconds of the first one was all she needed.

She saw a familiar room. And a familiar woman.

Ellis Ridgeway...

Disgust washed over her as she closed the files and closed the laptop. She unhooked the computer, pocketed the memory stick, and carried them both out of the office with her.

Behind the disgust came something else: uncertainty. Based on what she had seen on the laptop, maybe Windham *wasn't* the killer.

But even if he wasn't, he might potentially be something almost as bad.

CHAPTER TWENTY SIX

Mackenzie was drinking coffee and feeling a little irritated. Without Ellington by her side, she had no real interest in getting to know the officers that were sitting at the small conference table with her. Two of the three who had showed up at Windham's house were there—named Smith and Burke—as was the sheriff of Bedford.

She and the sheriff—a rotund man with the last name of Robinson on the nameplate on his chest—had watched snippets of the videos only after she had requested they do it in private, without any other officers. After watching enough (*more than enough,* if Mackenzie was being honest), she had called McGrath and told her what she had found. He seemed pleased and, given the nature of what was on the laptop, felt certain that once again, Mackenzie White had found her man. He then requested a full update after she interrogated him.

As she, Robinson, Smith, and Burke discussed the afternoon's events and what was on the movie files on the memory stick, she noticed that Sheriff Robinson looked pale. Like his officers, he wasn't really used to this sort of a mess, either. And while she knew that Clarke back in Stateton probably hadn't dealt with this sort of thing either, she found herself wishing this could have all plated out in Stateton. She felt like a nomad and it was wearing on her. She did her best not to let it show when she interacted with these new policemen, but she was pretty sure she was failing.

What she had discovered on the memory stick wasn't helping, either.

While she had wished for no more lurid content involving Kate Briggs, that wish had not been granted. Two of the movie files were home sex films, both featuring Kate. They were shot at a strange angle, fairly close to the bed. She assumed they had been filmed on Windham's phone and without Kate's knowledge.

That left nine movie files and they only got worse from there.

Seven of them showed footage from sterile-looking rooms. It wasn't until she saw the third one that Mackenzie recognized one of the resident rooms from the Wakeman Home for the Blind. More than that, she had also recognized the woman in the footage as Ellis Ridgeway.

Like the sex films, the footage had been filmed from inconspicuous angles. It was evident that the women in the footage had no idea they were being filmed. The quality of the films also made it clear that they had been edited. Windham had erased footage that was boring to him, keeping only footage that showed Ellis and four other women at four other locations, in various stages of undress. One of the films featured a young woman, perhaps in her early twenties, who seemed to be doing a bit of self-exploring as she lay in bed.

The third piece of footage was of Ellis Ridgeway, from Wakeman.

She was pretty sure the fifth was one of the rooms at the Mary Denbridge Home for the Blind in Richmond.

While she did not recognize the other women in the movies, she thought the pattern was clear. With the exception of the sex films with Kate Briggs, these were all women living in assisted homes for the blind.

"Ever seen anything like it before?" Robinson asked.

"Not quite like this, no," she answered. She was still a bit pissed from what she had discovered on the USB and that was bringing up the old anger of nearly being run down with a motorcycle. She was in a rotten mood and she was doing everything she could to remain professional.

"You think he's the one you're looking for?"

"I don't know yet," Mackenzie said, answering honestly. "I'll know after I talk to him, though."

"Well, he's all yours as far as I'm concerned," Robinson said, letting his disgust show clearly through.

Yes, he is, Mackenzie thought, equally disgusted.

And with that, she left the conference room and headed for the small interrogation room where Carl Windham had been waiting for the better part of an hour.

***

Windham still looked like the tormented man who had nearly crumpled in his kitchen, but Mackenzie could also see hints of the pushed-too-far man who had nearly put tire tracks between her eyes. The two sides of him seemed to be fighting for dominance as she entered the room. This time, the obstacle of the eye patch did not stop her from gauging his mood at all.

He looked annoyed when she entered the room and took the seat across from him at the wooden table near the back of the room.

"Why don't you tell me about the videos we found on a USB stick in your desk?" she asked.

He didn't flinch. She supposed he had assumed they'd find it. Still, he looked down to the table, a clear sign of shame. "They speak for themselves, don't they?"

"Yes, they do. And between you and me, you can talk about it with the police here in Bedford and some other agent at some point, I'd think. However, those videos and your past transgressions are not why I'm here. That's not why I came to speak with you."

"I know," he snapped. "You already told me that. You said Ellis Ridgeway is dead…that someone was targeting blind people. But that's not me."

She believed him, though not completely. There was something truly wrong with Carl Windham and she knew it would be foolish to dismiss him. But voyeurism did not always tie so neatly with the same sort of mental state that would lead someone to kill— especially blind people.

"I almost believe you," she said. "And for the sake of this conversation, let's just *pretend* that I believe you one hundred percent. You're guilty of secretly filming these defenseless blind women in their rooms and residences, but you're not a killer. Let's start from that playing field. That okay with you?"

He nodded, still finding it hard to look at her.

"One of the rooms I saw in your files looked very much like one of the resident room at the Mary Denbridge home in Chesterfield. Who is the woman in the video?"

"Vicki Connor," he said. "She's forty. Been blind all her life."

Mackenzie nodded and pulled out her phone. She texted Harrison a quick message that read: *Call Mary Denbridge Home ASAP. Make sure Vicki Connor is okay.*

"Did you read to her?"

"Yes. Sometimes. She enjoyed hearing the trashy stories in the tabloids. No books or anything like that."

"Did you have relationships with anyone else at the Mary Denbridge Home?"

"No. Just her."

"Did you come to know any of the residents in passing?"

"Not really."

"Does the name Wayne Nevins sound familiar to you?"

When he hesitated to think about it, Mackenzie was fairly certain that he was actually rummaging through a mental Rolodex. After a few seconds, he shook his head and looked up at Mackenzie finally.

"Is he another one?" he asked. "Another victim?"

"He is," she said. "There have been three so far, with a fourth attempted. So any information you can give me will help. And while I honestly doubt it can do much to sway law enforcement, it may help when your trial comes around."

She hated to use that ploy because, truth be told, she hoped Carl Windham got every solitary second of jail time due to him for what he had done to those poor women.

"What about Wakeman?" she asked. The anger was starting to flare back up and, quite frankly, she didn't want to push it down this time. "Did you read to more than one person there?"

"A few, actually," he said. "There was one named Becky Tosh. And another older woman named Nina Brady. And, of course, there was Ellis."

Well, I know for a fact that Nina Brady is alive and in no danger right now, she thought. *Unless he is the killer and he's marked her for later.*

"During your time as a volunteer with Guiding Sight, did you ever cross paths with any other volunteers?"

"Sometimes," he said.

"Anyone that stood out to you?"

He shook his head and looked back down at the table. "I never really tried getting to know them. I was too busy trying to hide what I was doing. I...I'm sorry, you know?"

He was close to weeping, but Mackenzie had no pity for him.

"Don't waste your fucking tears on me," she snapped. "Focus on my questions. You're certain?" she asked. "No one stood out?"

"No," he said, apparently gone rigid by the tone in her voice. "I'm sorry."

"What about other organizations?" Mackenzie asked. "When you volunteered for Guiding Sight, were there others you applied to?"

"No. But there's all kinds of volunteer opportunities. It's not always through an agency like Guiding Sight."

"Can you give me some examples?" Mackenzie asked.

"Well, yeah. I know for a fact that there's a service out of Lynchburg, through the big Christian college, where students do stuff like that for community service. I'm pretty sure there are all kinds of mission opportunities in smaller churches, too. That's what I hear, anyway. Shit...I know of people that needed to work off community service for speeding or parking tickets. Volunteers come from everywhere."

As Mackenzie cycled through all of this and sorted it out in her head, her phone buzzed at her. It was Harrison, prompt as usual. His reply text read: *Vicki Connor is doing just fine.*

Windham isn't the guy, she thought. *He's a creep and a pervert, but not a killer.*

She weighed her options. Should she tell McGrath right away or let him believe that a very likely suspect was being held in Bedford?

I need to get more names, she thought. *And this creep in front of me has a pretty good idea. Maybe it's not organizations I need to look at. Maybe it the more under the radar sort of volunteer opportunities…*

"That's it," she muttered under her breath as she got up from the table. "I'm done with you."

She didn't even bother looking back at Windham as she left the room. While she was now pretty sure he was not the killer, he was still not someone she wanted to be around. She knew that bringing someone like him to justice should be considered a small victory, but the fact that her killer was still on the loose robbed any joy out of the fact.

As she started to head into the small conference room at the end of the hall, her phone buzzed again. When it did, she looked at the time before anything else. Somehow, it had come to be 4:57 in the afternoon. That meant she had about fifteen hours remaining on McGrath's twenty-four-hour clock.

As her phone continued to buzz in her hand, she finally looked to the name in the display. It was Ellington, wanting to FaceTime with her.

She ignored it, pocketing her phone and hurrying to let Sheriff Robinson know that she was done with Windham. More than that, she was done with Bedford. She wasn't quite sure where she was headed from here—probably just the parking lot to formulate her next step—but she needed to be alone with her thoughts.

There was something just within her grasp now, especially after speaking with Windham. She felt that she was close but she couldn't grasp it. It was very much like the oppressive heat waiting for her outside—so present that it felt like you could reach out and grab it, only to come away with a handful of nothing.

CHAPTER TWENTY SEVEN

Before Mackenzie had time to get the rental car's air conditioning going properly, Ellington called again with another FaceTime request. She nearly ignored it again but then figured she should answer it just in case he had some sort of urgent message from McGrath or something about the case.

She accepted it and was a bit ashamed at how much good it did her heart to see his face. She tried to tell herself it was just because it was a friendly and loving face after the ordeal she'd recently been through—starting with having a soda can chucked at her head and ending with speaking face-to-face with a quite deranged Carl Windham.

"Hey," he said. And before she could say a single word, he was going on. Perhaps so she couldn't shoot him down right away— which she had fully intended to do. "Look, I know I screwed up. Not just with us, but professionally. That's why I...well, I didn't exactly head back to Quantico."

"Where are you, then?" she asked.

"Back in Richmond. I had planned on checking the Mary Denbridge Home but then got the word that you cracked the case. So...congrats, I guess. See...all it took was for me to leave you the hell alone for you to wrap this one up."

"Well, let's not get carried away. The guy I got—a particularly nasty guy named Carl Windham—is not our killer. I'm pretty certain of it."

"Well, shit. McGrath seems to think it's bottled up."

"Why'd he call you?" she asked.

He signed and shrugged. "He's still checking up on you. Progress reports."

Of course he is, she thought with disappointment. But that was a whole different issue to worry about at a later time.

"Anyway," Ellington said, "that's why I'm headed back up DC way in a bit. I thought we could meet up and return together. If you'll forgive me for acting like a heartbroken middle-schooler earlier."

"I'm not done yet," she said. "We still have about fifteen hours of the twenty-four he gave us."

"And I suppose you have an idea?"

The thing was that she *did* have an idea. It had come to her the moment Ellington and told her that she was in Richmond. But she wasn't sure she wanted him to know what it was. She was still

139

irritated with him and now that he had left her, she felt that it was *her* case.

That's pretty immature, she thought. *His help would come in handy, even if you don't want to admit it right now.*

"Hold tight for right now," she said. "I want you to do me a favor and call the Treston Home for the Blind and then the Mary Denbridge Home. It's going to be a pain in the ass, but I want you to ask for a list of every volunteer who has come in there in the last six months. They're smaller homes, so it shouldn't be too long of a list in either case."

"Okay," he said, interested. "And you?"

"I'm going to call Wakeman and then get in touch with Cleo Colegrove to see if she's hired any sort of outside help. Not even volunteers, per se…just someone to sort of assist. Then I'm going to call you and we're going to compare notes. Then…"

"…then the ones we have in common," he said, "we should be able to find pretty easily based on the organization they were with."

"Exactly."

"Let's do it," he said. "Call me when you're done."

She didn't even bother with a formal goodbye. She killed the call and instantly dialed Wakeman. Still a little disgruntled from her interactions with Carl Windham, she was short with the woman who answered the phone. She asked for Randall Jones directly, gave her name, and was patched through to him right away.

"Mr. Jones, I need you to do something for me. It could potentially be a waste of time, but I want to make sure the base is covered."

"Of course. What do you need?"

"I need the names of every single person that has volunteered there in the last six months. Not employees or payroll caretakers…just volunteers."

"Men *and* women?" Randall asked.

Mackenzie was pretty sure their killer was a man based on Cleo Colegrove's account, but she didn't see the point in taking any chances. "Yes, both, please. And I want you to read them to me over the phone. I'm sort if in a rush."

"Okay, yeah, I can do that. One second…"

She listened to him typing something into a computer, a few clicks, and then he cleared his throat.

"Okay, here we go. It's not that long of a list, and we're starting alphabetically."

Using a takeout napkin and a cheap pen from the glove compartment, Mackenzie jotted down the list of names. It took a little over four minutes and she had twenty-two names for her troubles—ten women and twelve men.

It was clear that Randall wanted to know what was going on without asking. But Mackenzie didn't have the time. More than that, with each name he gave her, the more certain she felt that this was going to work...that it was, in fact, something she and Ellington should have tried earlier.

But the volunteer connection wasn't quite as solid until earlier today, she thought. *There's no way we could have guessed.*

She then called Cleo Colegrove's cell phone number. No one answered but just as she was about to leave a message, Cleo called her back.

"Agent White," she said. "Any luck so far?"

"I don't know yet," she answered. "Look, I hate to trouble you, but I need to ask you about any caretakers you have. Is Maggie Reynolds the only person you have helping you?"

"Yes."

"What about the college courses you said you were taking? Is there any sort of special instructor that works closely with you or any of the other blind students?"

"Well, one of the classes is solely for blind students," she said. "But as for the other ones...no. Every now and then the instructor will catch me after class to make sure I don't feel like I'm at a disadvantage, but no. No special help."

"Has Maggie ever called in a relief worker of any kind?"

"No. If she's sick or needs to go somewhere, I'm on my own. But it's okay. I'm a big girl, after all."

"Indeed you are," Mackenzie said. "Thanks for your time, Cleo."

Again, she ended the call before the person on the other end had time to inquire about the purpose behind the call. She looked over her list from Wakeman one more time, making sure she gave Ellington ample time to place his two calls. Then, when she couldn't stave off the excitement any longer, she called him back. She opted for a simple voice call rather than a FaceTime chat.

He answered on the first ring. "Perfect timing," he said. "I just got off of the phone with the Mary Denbridge Home. I've got the two lists and the Treston one is pretty short. If you're ready, I'll give you the names."

"Shoot," she said.

Ellington read the names off and Mackenzie wrote them down in separate columns in small handwriting on the same napkin with the Wakeman list. The list of volunteers for Treston was only twelve people. The one for the Mary Denbridge Homes was considerably longer—longer even than the list of twenty-two she had gotten from Wakeman.

She studied the lists and when she saw a name more than once, she circled it.

"Got anything?" Ellington asked.

"One second," she said, still comparing the lists. It took her less than a minute and when she was done, she was a little amazed (and slightly frustrated) and what she saw.

Combining the lists, there were a total of sixty-three names.

Out of the three lists, nineteen names were circled twice; nineteen different people had volunteered for at least two of the homes.

But there were eight names that were circled in all three lists.

It's one of these names, she thought. But none of them were names that had come up in the investigation yet.

"Eight people," she said. "I've got two women and six men that have volunteered at all three of the homes."

"Holy shit. That can't be a coincidence, right?"

"Doubtful. Now I just need to know what agency they all went through in order to become volunteers."

"Okay, see," Ellington said, "this is where I make up for being such a dick this morning. The Treston list was only twelve people, so I went ahead and asked for the agencies that sent them."

"Good," she said, overlooking his meager little joke in hopes of a quick reconciliation. "Okay, so we'll start with the men because it just seems to fit the profile much easier. So, I need to know the places that sent the following names."

She recited the six names and by the time she was at the fourth one, Ellington was chuckling.

"What's funny?" she asked.

"I think we're finally catching a break," Ellington said.

"How so?"

"Three of those men were sent by the same agency. And two of them have known vision issues. The agency is called Reading the World."

"That's where we start, then."

"We?" he asked hopefully and with a bit of comedic flair.

"Yeah," she said. "Let's figure out the next—and hopefully *last* stop—and we'll meet up there."

He was about to say something else, probably something cute or charming, but she hung up before he had the chance.

And when she did it, there was a satisfied smile on her face.

She then placed another call, this one to Harrison in Quantico. "Harrison, I need you to get me a couple of addresses."

"For what, might I ask?" Harrison replied. He sounded tired and a little annoyed. In other words, very un-Harrison.

"Three more potential suspects."

Harrison paused and then started to make a *hmmm*ing noise. "I don't know, White," he said. "Look, McGrath already seems pretty pleased. Why push it? As far as he's concerned, you've wrapped the case up. Just call it a day and come on in."

"I can't. Not yet. I just need to make sure these names check out. If they do, I'll drop it and come in."

What she thought but did not say out of fear of pissing him off and losing his help was: *Yeah, and if the case* isn't *wrapped and we come back to DC and another blind person is killed in a few days, we'll all be eating humble pie.*

"Fine," Harrison said. He was almost sounding happy again. Desk jockey or not, she knew that he liked the excitement of a chase. "What are the names?"

She gave them to him and he gave a sigh. "Give me a few minutes."

"I can do that," she said, hanging up quickly yet again.

She felt like things were moving fast now, which was odd because she was sitting perfectly still in her rental car. It was infuriating to just have to wait. She spent the time doing her best to sort through the details, wanting to make sure she had everything in its right place before she headed out on the road again for a case that had already taken her all over the torturously hot state of Virginia.

The ordeal at Wakeman with the shoddy guestbook protocol is probably not isolated. One a volunteer gets established, known, and trusted, they can probably come and go without anyone batting an eye. So it has to be someone with a likeability factor.

Although, it also has to be someone so demented and focused on killing these people that he had the patience and drive to travel to each and every one of these homes. And it's not like they're all close to one another. That's a hell of a lot of driving...a hell of a lot of time fostering relationships, too.

But the Cleo Colegrove case doesn't really add up. He was desperate. Maybe cocky. But if he'd spent time getting to know the others, wouldn't he have spent time getting to know her? Or at least learn her routines?

The big question to all of this, of course, was *why?* She still expected the killer to have some sort of vision problem or to have been abused by someone with a vision problem in the past.

But the different homes is the curious aspect, she thought. *Why spread it out so far and wide? And why get to know them first? According to the caretakers at Wakeman, and Nina Brady, the volunteers were almost a staple. Familiar faces, friendly people that wanted to form relationships rather than just do a service and go home.*

"Forming relationships," Mackenzie said out loud.

There's something there, maybe. Something behind that...

Her phone rang, breaking her concentration. She was relieved to see that it was Harrison but also perplexed to see that she had been lost in her own thoughts for nearly ten minutes while he had acquired the information. All around the car, the afternoon was starting to grow dark. She glanced to the sky as she answered, seeing gathering thunderheads rather than the natural darkness of the coming dusk.

"What have you got?" she asked.

"And hello to you, too," Harrison quipped. "Okay, so this is a bit strange. But I guess it makes your job sort of easy. Two of these guys—Albert Rose and Lou Catron—live in the same town. A pretty small town from what I can tell. A place called Keysville. Seems fishy, doesn't it?"

"Absolutely. How about the other one?"

"Jason Torrence. Lives in Blacksburg, Virginia. He also just happens to own an enormous cattle farm and is heavily involved with the agriculture program at Virginia Tech. The guy has a ton of money and influence from what I can tell."

"Looks like I'll be heading to Keysville. Where the hell is that?"

"From what I'm seeing, it's about an hour and a half from Bedford, give or take a couple of minutes."

"Thanks, Harrison. Can you text me the exact addresses?"

"Sure, but—"

She cut him off by hanging up yet again. She backed out of the lot, her mind already whirling with ideas and possibilities.

Two volunteers from the same town, she thought. *Two volunteers that have been to all three of those homes...homes that are spread out all over the state. There's something to that, something...*

That's when it dawned on her. It was something Carl Windham had said. Maybe it wasn't an agency that had sent these guys.

Maybe it was some other sort of organization that sent people out to help others.

She then also thought of Robbie Huston and how he was so involved with certain ministries through his college.

Maybe these guys are part of a church, she thought. *Maybe they visited these homes as some sort of local mission project.*

I wonder if they're in it together...

If Ellington were with her, he'd be able to help her pry it all loose and stick it back together. They worked well together like that and he—

"Damn," she said, getting out her phone. In her excitement, she'd nearly forgotten to call him. She pulled up his number as she stopped at a stoplight, working her way out of Bedford's downtown district and back toward the four-lane road.

He answered quickly, as usual. "So where am I meeting you?" he asked.

"Keysville, Virginia. Two of the men on our list live there."

"That seems...odd. And promising. Oh, and get this. That Reading the World agency isn't an agency at all."

"It's church related, isn't it?"

"How the hell do you do that? Yes...it's a very small ministry in a very small church called Cornerstone Baptist. I saw it on the website just now."

"I think this is it," she said. "Look, I'm about an hour and a half out. You?"

"Closer to two hours, I think. Still...I think I could probably get there before you."

It's really hard to be mad at him, she thought with a smile.

"Doubtful," she said.

"Oh absolutely, I will. I could—"

She hung up on him for the second time in fifteen minutes. She would send him the address when Harrison sent it to her just to be fair. Yes...she was looking forward to having him back by her side and honestly not liking that even after less than a full day she realized how well they worked together and how much she missed him when he wasn't there.

Maybe we should *move in together,* she thought.

"One thing at a time," she told herself.

The light turned green and she pressed on. As the afternoon inched toward 6:30, the thunderheads continued to formed somewhere ahead of her. It was an ominous feeling, driving toward a place where she felt a killer might live while thunderheads grew in that direction.

But when she got the address via Harrison's text, she sped up. She'd battled the heat for the last several days. Those thunderheads might look foreboding, but there was likely rain in them.

Just another reason to head in that direction, she thought. It was the first time since arriving at the Wakeman Home for the Blind that she felt she was on the right track.

She continued on, the clouds growing darker as her foot grew heavier and heavier on the gas.

CHAPTER TWENTY EIGHT

The town of Keysville reminded Mackenzie quite a bit of Treston. It was a small and Rockwell-esque, complete with a pharmacy, white houses with white picket fences, and an honest to God barbershop with one of the candy stripe revolving poles out front. The barbershop and most of the other businesses were closed, though, as it was 8:32 when she guided the rental car down Main Street.

The drive had been constantly under the shadow of looming storm clouds and now that she was slowing on the residential streets, it seemed to catch up to her. Fat raindrops started to hit her windshield—one by one, as if the rain was slowly easing itself into the coming night.

True nightfall was probably another twenty minutes or so away but the storm clouds overhead did a fine job of faking it for the moment. In that fake nighttime darkness, Mackenzie double-checked the address and followed GPS directions. They took her off of Main Street and down a little side road. There, the houses got a little less cute, though they did still look like something from a Rockwell painting thanks to the eerie play of twilight colors courtesy of the storm clouds.

She arrived at the first address Harrison had sent her—the residence of Lou Catron—and then sent a text to Ellington to see where he was. Or…she *tried* sending the text. It was yet another small town where her coverage was terrible. She had one single bar that flickered in and out. The text to Ellington was stuck, waiting to find enough signal to be sent.

With a sigh, Mackenzie looked at the house. A beat-up truck sat in a cement driveway. The house looked innocent enough and she could tell that there was someone home; the telltale flickering light of a television could barely be seen through what she assumed was a living room window from the porch. She stepped out of the car and the humidity of the day felt different. There was a stillness in the air and a drop in temperature that nearly felt like a chill.

Thunder rumbled overhead. She could smell the storm coming. As she looked up the sky, a few raindrops pelted her in the face.

It's going to start raining soon, she thought. *And it's going to absolutely pour.*

Instinct told her to go ahead and get down to business. For some reason, the thought of walking to that front door in the midst of a storm was frightening. She slowly made her way to the porch and looked at the neighboring houses. The houses sat about twenty yards apart—not quite on top of one another but also not screaming privacy, either.

Before she reached the stairs, she checked her phone. The text to Ellington had still not gone through.

She made her way up the stairs, gingerly touching the side of her head. The attack from Carl Windham hadn't been a vicious one, but on the drive to Keysville, she'd noticed her head hurting where he had struck her with the ceramic bowl. She doubted there was much risk of a concussion but it still ached regardless.

Need to hurry, she thought. *If this guy doesn't pan out, I still have the other address—only three blocks away, but still…*

She raised her hand and knocked. Silence followed from the other side of the door. She leaned a little closer and realized that she could hear the muffled noise of the television. And then, behind that, a slight creaking. She thought it was the sound of feet tiptoeing toward the door. She waited a few more seconds and knocked again. The creaking stopped for a moment and then continued. It was broken up suddenly by a voice.

"Who's there?" the voice asked.

"FBI," she said.

And there it was. If the killer was on the other side of the door, he knew his game was up. The next five seconds or so would determine the way the rest of the night would go.

To her surprise, she heard the door unlocking from the other side. Her right hand went to her side, inches away from the Glock.

When the door opened, Mackenzie wasn't proud of the fact that she was momentarily shocked by what she saw. It was a man of about forty or so. The first thing she noticed was *not* the glass eye residing in his left eye socket. Instead, the first thing she noticed was the old scarring and misshapen state of the left side of his face.

But then her brain registered one of the very recognizable details Randall Jones and his caretakers had honed in on when describing volunteers who had come to the Wakeman Home for the Blind.

A glass eye…

She did her best to recover quickly. But she had left that small space for the man on the other side to speak first.

"FBI?" he said. "Um…what for?"

I don't want him thinking I got his name specifically, she thought quickly. *There's a good chance either he or a friend of his is the killer. Got to keep it vague as long as I can.*

"I'm working a case that led me to the name of a ministry at your church."

"And how do you know which church I attend?"

"Your name is Lou Catron, correct?"

Thunder rumbled behind her and now the sound of rainfall was steady and consistent. In the yard, on the road, on the roof of the house. Catron was momentarily frozen and she didn't think it was because the thunder had startled him.

"Cornerstone Baptist, right?" she said. "The ministry is Reading the World. I was given the names of everyone on the ministry. So I've been speaking with some of you for most of the afternoon. You just happen to be next on my list. Do you mind if I come in out of what looks to be a massive storm in the making to speak with you about it?"

He looked very uneasy. The scarring on his face and that still and featureless glass eye made him look eerie in the storm light. He eventually nodded and gave a weak, "Yeah, I guess."

Mackenzie kept her hand casually by her right hip where the Glock waited in its holster.

"Mr. Catron, I don't mean to alarm you, but there are many signs pointing to the fact that someone in your church might be responsible for at least three murders. More specifically, someone within the Reading the World ministry."

"Well, that's ridiculous," Lou Catron spat. "Also, it sounds like it's unfounded."

"No, I'm afraid it's not."

He had led her into a small den that sat adjacent to a smaller room where the television still whispered, showing a rerun of one of those clichéd hospital-related shows.

"Who else have you spoken to then?" he asked.

He's trying to deflect. He's not denying his church's involvement outright. He wants more names so he can pass blame if he needs to...

"I just came from Albert Rose's house," she said. "Please keep in mind, I am not accusing anyone of anything at this point. But I have to question everyone involved in that ministry. So...Mr. Catron, are you involved in Reading the World?"

He was standing by a doorway that led into a hallway. Mackenzie stood less than five feet from him, very aware that the doorway provided a quick escape if he decided to run. She could tell that he was deciding whether or not to be as truthful as he could or lie outright.

"Yes," he said finally. "It's a fine way to serve the community. And I find it hard to believe that anyone I serve with would be capable of murder. It's a little insulting, if I'm being honest."

"I'm sure it is," she said. "But like I said…it's just questioning at this point. What I am really looking for is anyone that has ever had any experience with volunteering at the Wakeman Home for the Blind in Stateton. Have you ever been there?"

Again, he hesitated before he answered but eventually said, "Yes. I've served there several times."

"And how did you serve?"

"Reading mostly."

"To who, exactly?"

Here, he paused again and this time she saw genuine worry on his face. When he looked to the floor with his one good eye and the glass eye remained stationary, it creeped her out. However, it also made the fear on his face easier to identify. Thunder rumbled outside, hard enough to rattle glasses in a kitchen she had not yet seen deeper in the house.

"I don't remember their names," he said.

He would not look at her. His hands were tucked in his pockets and she could tell that it was taking everything in him not to run.

"Are you sure?"

"Yes."

"Not even the name Alice Givens?" It was, of course, a fake name—the name of a girl she had played with as a kid.

She saw the relief on his face right away when he did not recognize the name. "No. I don't recall that name."

"How about Rebecca Wickline?" she asked, referencing a girl in high school that she had gotten drunk with after prom.

"No, not that one either," he said. The relief was like a mask on his face.

"And how about Ellis Ridgeway?"

The relief shattered and the recognition that took its place was impossible to miss. Catron actually leaned back against the doorframe at the sound of the name.

Got you, Mackenzie thought.

"No," he said. "Her either." But his voice was low and she should see the tremors in his knees.

She feigned frustration and sighed. She also relaxed her posture, hoping it would provide him with more relief. If she could catch him off guard like that one or two more times, that would be the end of it.

"How many homes for the blind have you visited through Reading the World?" she asked.

"A few," he said "Four, I guess."

"Have you ever been to Treston?"

He nodded. "Yeah. A small place. But the people up there are really nice."

"Did you ever meet a man named Kenneth Able when you were there?"

Without the cushion of fake names, the recognition in his face was the same expression someone may have if they were suddenly slapped in the mouth.

"What are you doing?" Catron asked. His voice was shaking a bit and he was slowly staring to inch away from the door frame and into the open space of the doorway itself.

"I'm looking for the man that killed three blind people and attacked a fourth," she said.

He shook his head back and forth slowly. In a way, he reminded her a bit of Carl Windham and the way he had responded when he knew she was on to him.

"Mr. Catron? Are you okay?"

"I…I had to," he said.

"Had to what?" she asked.

She could feel electricity in the air and she knew it was more than just the storm outside. She readied herself, prepared to move at the drop of a hat.

"You don't understand," Catron pleaded. "No one does."

"Then tell me," she said. "Help me understand."

Catron licked his lips and seemed to study the room. It was as if he was looking for other people, anyone else who might be there listening to him.

"I had to…I had to. I was blind, too. For a few months when I was a kid. My momma, she started it. She burned my eye out and…and…"

He screamed then and Mackenzie instantly went for her gun. When she realized that he was having a nervous episode that bordered on a panic attack, though, she eased up. Apparently, Catron saw this, too.

That's when he bolted. He whipped around the doorframe with speed that Mackenzie had not expected. The hallway beyond was dark, barely illuminated by the light from the den in which she currently stood.

She drew her Glock and took three steps toward the doorway. "Mr. Catron, don't make this hard on yourself. It sounds like you have some problems. And if you *have* done something you regret, you can talk to someone. Start with me. Let me help…"

She had no interest in helping, really. But she could tell from that way he had pleaded with her that she would have to pretend to be sympathetic if she hoped to bring him out of the hallway without any physical confrontation.

He did not respond, though. So with her muscles tensed with adrenaline and every bit of training coming to the forefront of her mind, she stepped to the doorway. She peered into the darkness ahead before stepping through. She saw three doors—two mostly closed and one wide open. Catron was nowhere to be seen.

She stepped forward, through the doorframe and into the hallway. Up ahead, something glimmering caught her eye. It was a chandelier, made of paper, its long strings dangling and shimmering, catching the light in a confusing way.

She saw his fist just a split second before it struck her between the eyes, and she knew the fixture had been meant to confuse. The bastard had been hiding behind the doorframe, waiting to pounce.

She stumbled backward, and for the second time in three hours, black flecks rocketed across her vision. And before she had the chance to blink them away, she sensed Catron blasting by her. His shoulder struck her right side and she went spinning against the wall.

He's not attacking now, though, she thought. *He's retreating.*

She blinked the pain away and as she tried following after him, toward the living room, she noticed that she was seeing a hazy double image to everything. She took a step forward and felt dizzy. She then closed her eyes for a moment, collected her wits, and opened them again. The double vision was gone and when she stepped forward, the dizziness had subsided.

She instantly took a shooter's stance, going low and creeping toward the living room. A quick glance at what she could see of the room revealed that the only way out was into the den. From there, he'd have access to the rest of the house or the front door. But he had to go through her first.

So why the hell did he go in there?

Her answer came in what she thought was the booming of thunder at first. But then she saw Catron running from behind the cover of the small couch, a pistol in his hand.

At the same moment, she felt like something in her left shoulder had started to leak. It was followed by a dull stinging sensation and that's when she realized she'd been shot.

She raised her gun at the fleeing shape of Catron and fired one round, then another. She didn't know if she hit him or not because the world had gone into the double-vision mode again. She saw his moving shape, but that was it. He might as well have been a shadow. She fired a third shot, knowing she missed but feeling the need to do so anyway.

She heard the front door open and the sound of rain filled the house.

She quickly looked at her left shoulder. She'd been shot, but it was only a graze. If she took the time, she was sure she'd find the bullet lodged in the wall behind her—maybe with the fabric of her shirt and some of the flesh from her shoulder affixed to it.

A spike of frustration roared through her and it seemed to wash away the haze of the pain in her head and shoulder. She took a deep breath and headed for the open door. She did so with caution, refusing to fall victim to a cheap shot from around corner as she had moments before.

But thanks to the last waning fragments of rain-shrouded evening light, she could see Catron's shape moving through the front yard. He was running for the small truck she had seen upon arriving.

She hurried to the porch, growing dizzy as she moved faster. She reached the porch railing and leaned against it to steady her arm. She took aim, her left shoulder complaining to no end, and fired.

Her shot rang true, taking out Catron's left knee. He screamed as he fell to that knee. He was propped up against the truck, leaning against it for support. As he fell, he also wheeled around and fired off another shot of his own. Mackenzie ducked down at the sound. It went wide right and would have missed her anyway. The shot tore a gouge of wood out of the frame of the front door.

She took aim again and fired back, not wanting to kill him but to incapacitate him. She saw that he had opened the driver's side door now. He was using it as a shield as he climbed inside.

Mackenzie got to her feet but stayed low as she went toward the stairs. She fired at the truck now, not trusting herself to shoot at Catron's upper body without killing him. She took out both front tires and then put two rounds in the truck's grille, hoping they'd do some damage under the hood.

Immediately following her final shot, Catron returned with one of his own. This one was also wide, tearing a spindle along the porch railing in half.

Mackenzie went down the stairs, the rain doing nothing to help her hazy vision.

"Drop your weapon, Mr. Catron!"

They looked at one another through the driver's side door. Rain splattered the window as he shut the door.

I'm going to have to shoot him again. And if it kills him...

Suddenly, he started the engine and began to take off.

Mackenzie tried to get a clean shot—without killing him—but it was impossible.

She was about to run into the way of the pickup—a daring move that would probably get her injured—when there came the sound of another approaching engine. It roared up to Catron's house and swerved hard into the driveway. It was a black Ford Focus that she had never seen before. It pulled up directly in front of Catron's truck, blocking its path—and forcing Catron to slam into it.

The Focus took a hard hit, leaning sideways, almost flipping. But then it righted as the truck's wheels got stuck in the fresh mud.

Mackenzie was surprised and relieved to see Ellington stumble out of the car, dazed, raising his gun to train it at Catron's truck.

Carlton, though, had the jump on him. He recovered faster from the collision, raised his gun, and aimed it right at Ellington.

"Don't move, asshole," Mackenzie said firmly and coldly into his ear, just inches behind him. She had taken the opportunity to creep up around him get in the passenger's side, and now she had her gun shoved hard against his neck.

He must have gotten the point, because she saw his eye widen with terror, then watched him slowly drop his gun.

Barely had he done so than she reached up, grabbed his wrists, and snapped them behind his back, cuffing him.

He whimpered, slumping over in his seat, realizing it was all over.

Mackenzie let out a sigh of relief.

Ellington rushed forward, doing everything he could to not seem as out of sorts as he was.

"You okay?" Ellington asked.

She grinned, studying his Focus, turned halfway on its side.

"Shouldn't I ask you the same question?" she said.

They both smiled at each other, as thunder sounded and the rain poured down harder than ever.

Finally, the storm had broken.

CHAPTER TWENTY NINE

While Mackenzie had managed to avoid a concussion at the hands (and ceramic bowl) of Carl Windham, she *had* suffered one from Lou Catron's right fist. She'd also received several stitches in the shoulder from the errant shot from Catron's gun. She'd been vaguely aware of all of this following a brief blackout in Catron's front yard and coming in and out of wakefulness in the back of an ambulance.

In her short hospital stay, Ellington filled her in on what he'd gathered from the interrogation process after Catron had been brought in.

"Ironically, the nearest prison was in Stateton," Ellington said. "When Clarke saw Lou Catron, I thought his head was going to explode. Clarke knew him—not well, but in that small-town way everyone knows everyone else, you know? Given that the bastard had tried killing you and had no qualms about shooting at people, I was honestly expecting a hell of a fight. But after we got him into that little interrogation room, he seemed to know it was over. And he told us everything."

She pondered everything, the maniacal look in his eye, his crazed words. She realized he must have been terribly abused as a boy, and somehow he carried this vendetta throughout his life. Paradoxically, he'd targeted blind people, even though he himself had been made blind by his mother. In a way, she realized, he was not only filled with hatred toward her, but toward himself. He blamed himself for what had happened to him.

And so he targeted people like him.

"He killed his mother, didn't he?" she finally asked.

Ellington looked back at her, surprise in his eyes.

"Yes. How did you know?"

"The way he spoke about her," she said. "How long ago?"

Ellington sighed.

"He's not sure. But we had a few guys at the bureau look into his claims and they seem to check out. Somewhere around twenty-five years ago, Deborah Catron went missing. That's all anyone knows for sure. But Lou Catron told us where be buried her very badly mutilated body. And it checked out. They found it within four hours of Lou telling them. He killed his high school girlfriend, too. But he couldn't remember where he dumped the body."

Mackenzie processed all of this. There was something eerie about knowing the killer she had helped to stop had been killing long before he'd taken Kenneth Able's life, and no one had had any idea.

"He started looking for ways to get into places where blind people stayed," Ellington continued. "That's why he started attending Cornerstone Baptist; he heard about Reading the World."

"And they just let him in?"

"Yeah. I talked to the pastor and some of the congregation myself. They were shocked. Lou Catron was apparently a stand-up guy from what they could see. He played them well, it seems."

"But...wait. What about Cleo Colegrove? She wasn't in a home."

"Catron says he was looking into ministries in Lynchburg since there's such a huge religious community up there. He was hoping to get into more homes for the blind, some out of state. While he was there, someone told him to check with an instructor that was volunteering as a teacher for tech courses for the blind. He saw Cleo there and apparently..."

He sighed.

"He's not showing any remorse."

She wasn't surprised.

They sat there for a long time in the silence, processing it all.

Finally, Ellington surprised her by leaning in and kissing her softly on the mouth. When he pulled away, he added: "It's done. You got him. You nearly died, but you got him."

She nodded and this time it was she who initiated the kiss. This one was longer and lingered a bit.

When she was done, she looked at him thoughtfully. "Can I ask just one more question?"

He rolled his eyes. "I suppose."

"Do you still want to move in together?"

He didn't answer right away. Not with his words, anyway. He started with his hands and then with the rest of his body.

***

When Mackenzie returned to work two days later, most of her afternoon had consisted of a stern talking-to from McGrath. He had to. But when he was done, she noticed his small smile and his clear look of admiration. She would be on desk duty for at least two weeks while she recuperated and the details of her altercation with Lou Catron were properly looked into.

She was fine with that. Honestly, she would have happily accepted more desk time. She was still shaken by the scene at

Catron's house—more than she was willing to admit to Ellington and certainly to McGrath.

Besides, at her desk she would be able to devote more time to the case that had been in the back of her mind for the last two months: her father's case, which had been reopened and was currently active (yet buried under countless others) back in Nebraska. It would give her more time to reconnect via the phone with Kirk Peterson, the detective who was doing his best to stay on the case even as it turned colder and colder by the day.

She knew she'd eventually have to return to Nebraska if she hoped to ever find closure on the case. It was a wretched feeling, almost like planning to attend her own funeral. But she knew she'd never have true peace until it was all behind her.

Following that first day back and the lackluster meeting with McGrath, Mackenzie left the building alone. She'd be going to her own apartment, but only for another few days. Ellington had been sent back down to Keysville, Virginia, to follow up with members of Catron's church and after that, he'd be traveling to Bedford to tie up a few loose things with the Carl Windham case. After that, they would start moving her into his apartment.

And from there...well, who knew?

Mackenzie walked across the parking lot, toward her car. She was busy thinking about what the move might be like and how it would ultimately change their relationship...and that's why she didn't notice the white rectangle on her windshield until she was right up on her car.

There was a piece of paper on her windshield, tucked between the wiper and the glass.

No, not just a piece of paper.

A business card.

Her breath caught in her throat as she slowly reached out for it. Even before she freed it, she knew what she'd find there. When she plucked it away from the wiper, she was not at all surprised to find out that she was right.

The front of the business card read **Barker Antiques**.

A chill raced through her as she turned the card over in her hand. On the back, a brief message had been scrawled in thin cursive handwriting.

Stop looking.

With the business card still in her hands, Mackenzie scanned the parking lot. She saw a few of her co-workers headed for their cars but no one suspicious. She then looked for any figures sitting in their cars, looking displaced or out of the ordinary. But she saw nothing of the sort.

She slowly got into her car and started the engine. Before pulling away, she studied the card again.

Stop looking.

Mackenzie pocketed the card and backed out of her parking spot. The move into Ellington's apartment was suddenly the last thing on her mind.

Stop looking.

With a stern look of defiance on her face, two different words came out of her mouth.

"Like hell," she said.

She headed home with her father's case looming large in her mind, pushed by the certainty that she would no longer be able to accurately perform the duties of her job until this fragmented piece of her past was put behind her.

BEFORE HE SINS
(A Mackenzie White Mystery—Book 7)

From Blake Pierce, bestselling author of ONCE GONE (a #1 bestseller with over 900 five star reviews), comes book #7 in the heart-pounding Mackenzie White mystery series.

In BEFORE HE SINS (A Mackenzie White Mystery—Book 7), priests are turning up dead, their bodies found crucified against church doors throughout Washington, D.C. Could this be some sort of act of revenge? Could it be a member of their order? Or a serial killer, hunting priests with a far more diabolical motive?

The FBI turns to special agent Mackenzie White, as the case bears a resemblance to the religious overtones of her first case, The Scarecrow Killer. Plunged into the subculture of the priesthood, Mackenzie struggles to learn more about the rituals, about ancient scripture, to try enter the killer's mind. But Mackenzie is already preoccupied by her hunt for her father's own murderer, determined to find him this time. And this new killer is more sinister than most, and will push her, in his deadly cat and mouse game, to the very brink of her own sanity.

A dark psychological thriller with heart-pounding suspense, BEFORE HE SINS is book #7 in a riveting new series—with a beloved new character—that will leave you turning pages late into the night.

Also available by Blake Pierce is ONCE GONE (A Riley Paige mystery—Book #1), a #1 bestseller with over 900 five star reviews—and a free download!

Blake Pierce

Blake Pierce is author of the bestselling RILEY PAGE mystery series, which includes ten books (and counting). Blake Pierce is also the author of the MACKENZIE WHITE mystery series, comprising six books (and counting); of the AVERY BLACK mystery series, comprising five books; and of the new KERI LOCKE mystery series, comprising four books (and counting).

An avid reader and lifelong fan of the mystery and thriller genres, Blake loves to hear from you, so please feel free to visit www.blakepierceauthor.com to learn more and stay in touch.

BOOKS BY BLAKE PIERCE

RILEY PAIGE MYSTERY SERIES
ONCE GONE (Book #1)
ONCE TAKEN (Book #2)
ONCE CRAVED (Book #3)
ONCE LURED (Book #4)
ONCE HUNTED (Book #5)
ONCE PINED (Book #6)
ONCE FORSAKEN (Book #7)
ONCE COLD (Book #8)
ONCE STALKED (Book #9)
ONCE LOST (Book #10)

MACKENZIE WHITE MYSTERY SERIES
BEFORE HE KILLS (Book #1)
BEFORE HE SEES (Book #2)
BEFORE HE COVETS (Book #3)
BEFORE HE TAKES (Book #4)
BEFORE HE NEEDS (Book #5)
BEFORE HE FEELS (Book #6)

AVERY BLACK MYSTERY SERIES
CAUSE TO KILL (Book #1)
CAUSE TO RUN (Book #2)
CAUSE TO HIDE (Book #3)
CAUSE TO FEAR (Book #4)
CAUSE TO SAVE (Book #5)

KERI LOCKE MYSTERY SERIES
A TRACE OF DEATH (Book #1)
A TRACE OF MUDER (Book #2)
A TRACE OF VICE (Book #3)
A TRACE OF CRIME (Book #4)

Made in the USA
Monee, IL
26 February 2021